THE
QUIETUDE
OF CALVARY

Jamison Whiteman

To my parents, Paul and Elizabeth Whiteman, and parents-in-law, Louis and Eleanor Saghy, in memory. Members of the greatest generation that America has ever seen.

Prologue

Jerusalem, 33 A.D.

In the seventh year of Pilate's term as Prefect of the Roman Province of Judea, during the nineteenth year of the reign of Emperor Tiberius, a rabbi from Nazareth named Jesus was to be crucified. According to His accusers, Jesus had been preaching throughout Jerusalem, claiming to be the king of the Jews. Under Roman law, claiming to be a king was a capital crime, so death by crucifixion was ordered.

*****

As Jesus was being led to His crucifixion, His path was halted innumerable times by the taunts, jeers, insults, and physical abuses of those lining the street and witnessing this execution. Although Scripture and Tradition teach us that there were many instances of those who mourned and lamented Him, and there are many instances of those who attempted to comfort and aid Jesus on this *Via Dolorosa*, He was still subjected to tremendous abuse. History has shown that crucifixion, a form of capital punishment that became common under Alexander the Great, was considered to be one of the most horrible and disgraceful forms of execution. The victim would be nailed, or in many instances, tied to a cross and left to hang until death occurred due to heart failure or asphyxiation. Before victims were crucified, they were beaten and tortured and then forced to carry their cross to the site of their execution. Up until the last moments of crucifixion, victims were still berated and reviled by the crowd. On many occasions, the crowd tore the person down from the cross and beat the victim to death. But in the last few moments of the crucifixion of Jesus, unlike most crucifixions, the crowd became incredibly quiet as darkness fell upon the whole land. This stillness of the crowd and the events leading up to it provide the basis of our story.

Chapter One

The Present Day
Jet Propulsion Lab (JPL), Pasadena, CA

Murray Edgeton, Ph.D. at age twenty-six, was the most gifted scientist at NASA's JPL. Even comparing him to the most significant names in physics: Albert Einstein, Niels Bohr, Werner Heisenberg, Arthur Eddington, and others, he was one of the brightest physicists to ever walk into a lab. At least, that's what the scientific community thought about him. He had been working at the Jet Propulsion Laboratory for the past three years, and he was on the cusp of validating the theory he had worked on since his time at the Massachusetts Institute of Technology, MIT. While pursuing his doctorate in physics at MIT, his main area of research had been furthering the work of his hero, Albert Einstein. He was expanding on Einstein's theory of relativity, specifically as it pertained to the Space-Time Continuum.

Murray was very fortunate to have Dr. Ignatius Joseph, called 'Nate' by his colleagues, a particle physicist working with him on his research. Nate had been involved in the latest research on the quark substructure of matter. During the past year, he had developed a strong but unlikely personal and professional relationship with Murray. Professionally, the two physicists had similar goals concerning their research, and they also had similar philosophies regarding the role of science, but their personal beliefs could not be more different. Murray was an avowed atheist and was very outspoken in his atheistic and anti-theistic views. Conversely, Nate was a very devout Syro-

Malabar Rite Catholic from the state of Kerala in southern India. While Murray was very outspoken in his views and would vocally profess his negative opinions on the existence of a Supreme Being, Nate would very calmly and persuasively present his. Watching these two intellects banter back and forth was maddening to those who worked with them. Despite their conflicting views of religion, Drs. Edgeton and Joseph felt as if they complemented each other's work.

While reviewing their research's latest computer analysis, Nate asked his colleague, "Well, what do you think? The results from this latest simulation look quite promising. At this point, we have enough data to bring to the National Academy of Science and The Griffith Group to ask for funding."

"I think that we do, too. The last run made me a bit nervous, but it looked as if the data could show significant correlation and predictability to our hypotheses. Yeah, we have enough. I'll have my office contact the NAS and Griffith to see if we can get something on the calendar. This past year has gone by too quickly, but I can feel it, Nate. We're almost there. We need to make a few more tweaks to this, and I was hoping to have Jill take another look at our findings. I don't want to go with our hat in hand to this meeting and not have everything lined up perfectly. We've got a chance to use Lawrence Livermore's Blue Gene/P this weekend, and I'd like Jill to have a run at the numbers with their supercomputer. Are you able to join us?"

"Thanks, Murray," he replied. "We have a baptism to go to for my wife's nephew, so we won't be available unless you need me."

"No, no worries, Jill and I can take this." Shaking his head, Murray continued, "So, you have another one of those religious things this weekend. I know I've been saying this for a while, Nate, but I can't understand how you all can give credence to that stuff."

Nate just smiled at his friend. "You'll figure it out one of these days. In the meantime, I'll keep you in my prayers."

"Yeah, right, lot of good that will do me."

Laughing with each other at their ongoing banter, they walked out of Murray's office and down the hall to Dr. Jill McAllister's office. Jill was from Statesboro, Georgia, and she was one of the staff members at the JPL. She received her Ph.D. in mathematics from Georgia Tech and was known for her work in chaos theory. She had been involved with an ad hoc group working in concert with Murray and Nate, and she was going to help review the data from their last computer simulation. She was reviewing a printout of their computer run when Murray and Nate walked into her office.

"Hey, Jill," Murray said upon entering her office. "Looks as if you've got the results of our last computer run. What do you think?"

Looking up from her desk and smiling, Jill replied, "Oh, hi Murray, hi, Nate. You'll have to give me a bit more time on this, but the results look pretty solid at first glance." She let out a low whistle, "Wow. How long did it take to run all of these data? There are billions of calculations here, unbelievable."

Murray smiled back at her, "It looks as if you'll get to see for yourself this weekend if you're up for it. I have another crack at Livermore's Blue Gene/P this Saturday, and I was going to head up tomorrow to set things up. Are you game?"

"Sure, I'd love to see that thing at work. It'll be just three of us, right? Anyone else heading up with us?"

"No, just you and me. Nate has one of those voodoo sessions this weekend, so he'll be staying down here."

"You really are a heathen, Murray," Nate laughed while shaking his head. "Jill, my wife's nephew is having his infant son baptized this weekend, so we have a family party planned. Sorry that I can't make it up there with the two of you, but doing one more validation of our model will help with our presentation to the Academy."

Murray jumped in, "Speaking of which, I have to get my admin assistant to get ahold of Washington to get us on the calendar for a meeting with the Academy. Jill, can we meet up later this afternoon to do some planning before we head up tomorrow for this weekend's run? I can get some flights up to San Jose and then get us a couple of rooms up there; what do you think? Can we shoot for 4:00?"

"I'll see you at four, my office or yours, Murray?" she replied.

"Let's meet at my office. See you both later on." Murray turned and left.

Jill closed the door behind Murray. "I know it's none of my business, Nate, but I don't know how you put up with Murray's constant digs at you and your faith. I know you're a spiritual man, and your faith is very important to you. I don't know how you can just laugh it off."

Nate replied, "Jill, his constant digs, as you say, don't bother me. I just let it roll off my back. Back home in India, there is a lot of religious animosity that turns violent way too much, so his little jabs at me are nothing. I pray for him as I know that something is bothering him deep down. I've worked with several colleagues who have agnostic or atheistic views, and they never bring the issue of my spiritual life up at all. It's just Murray. Something must have happened to him in the past; he just hasn't opened up, but I'm working on it. But back to what we were talking about earlier, what do you think of Murray's project?"

"It's a fascinating premise, I will grant you that. As a mathematician, I always try to reduce everything to polynomial equations. I feel that the language of mathematics can explain everything, but Murray's theory is pretty wild. I'm looking forward to seeing the Blue Gene/P supercomputer and looking at the data again. Murray mentioned that he may want me to be more involved with your research as he wants to get a formal team put together to continue working on his theory. Has he mentioned this to you?"

"Yes, he did. I've recommended that Murray consider adding some other disciplines to this group; we need to have some ethicists added to our team, and I think you can see why. The consequences for this project are much more than simply 'significant;' they're monumental, and they could be a species-ending event, specifically for us. We need to discuss and flesh out what we are doing and develop a set of comprehensive parameters and guidelines. What do you think?"

Jill replied, "I agree with you, Nate, and for a start, I recommend that you two start looking at chaos theory. The reasons are pretty obvious."

Nate nodded his head; the reasons were pretty obvious. Murray's work demonstrated that time travel is possible, and his goal was to find a way to make it a reality.

.

Danville, California

Murray and Jill flew to San Jose and then drove their rental car to Livermore, CA, home of the Lawrence Livermore National Laboratory, LLNL. The LLNL describes itself in its mission statement as "a premier research and development institution for science and technology applied to national security." As a federal research facility, they had an agreement with NASA's JPL to provide technical support to Murray's research project. They had rooms at a hotel in Danville, a small upscale community near the LLNL, where they would stay until their return to Pasadena following the computer run. They would have a working dinner that evening and then spend the following day at the lab.

As he was getting ready for his dinner with Jill, Murray stared at his image in the mirror. He was, by all accounts, a very handsome man. His mother's beauty and his father's good looks passed through to him as he won the genetic sweepstakes for physical attractiveness. He was still relatively young and had never been married. He had several girlfriends in college but never dated seriously. This wasn't due to a lack of opportunities or admirers. He felt that romantic entanglements distracted him from his life's work. He had some friends when he was in school at the Massachusetts Institute of Technology, and within that circle of friends, he knew a number of young women. He worked in study groups with them, and they would go to the typical college hangouts. He became serious with one of the girls in the group, and they dated off and on for about a year. His girlfriend, Mia Zolezzi from Bergen County, New Jersey, was studying chemistry, and they enjoyed each other's company, both socially and academically. By the time they graduated from MIT, their romance had ended, and they had both moved on, Murray to his doctoral program and Mia to an internship with Dupont.

But as he looked at himself in the mirror, he found himself thinking of his Jill. He realized that she was a bit more than just a colleague. They had spent a lot of time together working on his project, and it surprised him to realize that thinking about her made his heart rate bump up just a bit. He mused to himself, "Get a grip, Murray, she's just a colleague," but something in the back of his mind told him that along with being incredibly bright, Jill was also very nice-looking. He found himself looking forward to dinner with Jill.

*****

Jill was getting ready for her working dinner with Murray in the adjoining suite. Like Murray, she was an academic who did not care about being involved romantically. She, too, felt that it distracted her from her work. Jill was an extremely attractive woman, but she never paid attention to her physical attributes, as her work consumed all of her time. Her friends would tell her how pretty she was, but she didn't see the relevance of being attractive. She told herself that if it didn't help her with her work, what was the sense? But that evening, as she was getting ready for dinner, she found herself looking forward to seeing him in a setting outside of the workplace. She found her time with Murray to be academically very stimulating, but there was something more, she could feel it. She heard some of the gossip around the proverbial water cooler about how "hot" Murray was. Looking at him through a different lens, she thought they were right. He was certainly handsome, but she didn't know much about him outside of his research. She looked at herself one more time in the mirror, and then she thought, "*Who are you kidding?* He *doesn't see anything in you other than a math whiz.*" But then she also heard a little voice asking her, "Why not? We're both highly intelligent professionals and hold many of the same interests. Why couldn't we become involved romantically? Individuals of our species have been doing this for years. I'm no different, am I?" She had to shake her head to clear her thoughts. She asked the mirror, "I'm right. Who am I kidding?" But that didn't stop her from paying more attention to her hair and make-up than usual. As she walked out the door, she found herself looking forward to having dinner with Murray. "What I'm really looking forward to is having him look at me and see *me.*" With that, she headed to the elevator.

Dinner that evening started off a bit differently than they expected. Although they didn't pick this up in each other, they were both nervous and anxious. They were dressed casually, California dining being what it was, and the first thing that Jill noticed was that Murray stood for her as she arrived at the table. He wore a pair of Lee jeans and cowboy boots; she had never seen him like this. She thought, *"Well, he is from Texas, after all, but what a nice change."*

Murray, for his part, was looking at her differently, "this is almost like a date," he said to himself, and he noticed that Jill just wasn't very nice looking; she was spectacularly beautiful. He had never seen this before. And the way she was dressed, if she were looking to surprise him, she was doing a great job of it. She wore designer jeans and a sweater that showed off her incredible shape. He was stunned.

"Close your mouth, Murray. You look as if you've never seen a woman before." She tapped the bottom of his chin to close his mouth as she laughed. Noticing that he stood for her when she arrived, she said, "Thank you, Murray. I guess you did learn proper manners in Texas," as she sat down.

"Sorry, Jill, you just caught me by surprise, that's all. I've never seen you outside of work, and it's nice to know that there is another side to you. I also need to apologize because I said this would be a working dinner, but I must have spaced it out. I left all of my work in the room. Can you hold on for a second?

I can run back up and get everything."

She pulled him back as he began to walk away, "No, please don't worry about it. We never have the opportunity to talk as two friends from work, so let's enjoy ourselves for a change. We can catch up on work tomorrow morning and come down for an early breakfast and talk shop. Sound OK? Please have a seat, and let's look at the menu." She was surprised at herself; her anxiety was gone, and she felt as if someone else were occupying her body.

"That sounds great. I tell you what, I could enjoy a beer right about now. Can I get you something to drink?" he asked.

"I'd like that. We are close to wine country up here; I'd like to try one of the wines from Napa Valley."

Almost on cue, their waiter approached their table and asked if he could get them anything to drink from the bar. Murray replied, "Thank you. Jill, would you care for anything to start off?"

"I would like to see your wine list. I'm interested in trying something from Napa Valley. Let me ask you what you recommend."

Their waiter, James, replied, "I would like to let you know that we have quite a few vineyards here in the Livermore Valley; you may know that the Livermore Valley is California's original wine country. We have two very good vintners that I'd like to recommend, 'The Windows Winery,' and a new up-and-coming vintner, 'The Little Post Vineyard.' They have some excellent selections that you might enjoy."

James and Jill got into a good discussion of the various wines in the area, and then James asked Murray, "And you, sir, what might I get for you?"

"How about an IPA? I'm really sophisticated."

The evening took off from there. Over drinks, they talked briefly about their upcoming meeting at the LLNL, but then she steered the conversation towards themselves and away from work. "Tell me about yourself, Murray. We always talk about work, but I have to say that I do not know that much about you besides the fact that you're from West Texas and that you went to MIT. What else can you tell me about the mysterious Dr. Edgeton?"

"There is nothing mysterious about me, Jill. Just your typical hard-working boy from Texas who got lucky and went to MIT. How about you?"

Smiling at Murray's answer and how neatly he sidestepped her question, she told him about herself. "My mom and dad come from families with deep Georgia roots. My mom is a Daughter of the American Revolution. We have quite a few DARs down in Georgia. My dad is an engineering professor at Georgia Tech, the top engineering school in America," Murray smiled at her. "I have a sister who is a veterinarian and a brother who is a classical guitarist, but to be honest, he is a professional bum. He has not worked a single day after graduating from Vanderbilt with a degree in music. Mom and Dad keep letting him get away with it, so what can I say? Besides that, I have been working with JPL for three years, just like you. I lead a very ordered and somewhat boring life," smiling as she said that.

Murray sat there for a moment and then opened up a bit. "I never met my father, and my mother was a waitress at a diner back home. We lived in an old single-wide trailer, and as the old expression goes, 'If it cost a dollar to go around the world, we wouldn't have enough to get to the bus depot.' How's that for a little Dickensian story as we sit in this nice little restaurant in a beautiful setting drinking exceptional wine and an incredible IPA."

Jill remembered how Nate mentioned something about Murray being hurt when he was younger. She was beginning to see his veneer crack just a bit and was hoping that she could slip into that narrow opening. During dinner, they talked about things they hadn't shared with anyone at work, but he didn't talk anymore about his past. After a nice dinner, she took his arm, and they headed to the elevator and back up to their rooms.

"Jill, I've had a very nice time with you this evening, but let me get you the outline for our meeting tomorrow morning; maybe you can take a quick look at it before we meet for breakfast tomorrow. Is that all right with you?"

She answered, "Sure, no problem. I have a difficult time sleeping in a hotel, and this might knock me out." They laughed, "If I have any questions, I'll just knock on our adjoining door." Murray went into his room, got the folder, and handed it to Jill, and with that, they wished each other good night.

As Jill walked into her room, she thought, *"Well, that was a letdown. I thought that we would have more of a chance to talk; he was beginning to open up to me."* But she got herself ready for bed and started reading Murray's outline. The longer she read the outline, the more she realized she was upset that their evening didn't turn out how she hoped it would. Getting out of bed and throwing the hotel robe over her negligee, she opened her side of the adjoining door and knocked.

Murray was in his room thinking along the same lines. He enjoyed working with Jill and found her to have an incisive and brilliant mind, but tonight, he noticed for the first time that she was gorgeous. He asked himself again, *"How come I never saw this before?"* He also found himself thinking about her nonstop. As he got undressed and put on a pair of sweatpants, he heard a knock on his door. "She can't be done already?" But he was happy to hear her knock on the door, and he noticed that his heart was racing. Opening the door, he saw Jill standing there with an interesting look on her face. She looked down and saw that Murray was responding to her presence. With a knowing smile, she handed him the folder. Trying to hold back her laughter at Murray's discomfort, she told him, "I took a quick look at this, and it looks good. Let's review this again in the morning unless you want to talk about it now."

His mouth was dry, and he cursed himself. Looking at her made his heart do flip-flops, and his body responded. Little Murray appeared to wake up and start stretching at a most inopportune time. He reached for the folder to take it from her, but she held on to it. He pulled on the folder, and she followed. The next thing they knew was that the folder dropped to the floor, spilling papers everywhere. He took her in his arms, and they threw their clothing on the floor as they made their way to his bed.

Later, lying in each other's arms, she looked up at him. "That was incredible. I never knew it could be so enjoyable. How are you feeling?"

He looked at her and was struck by how beautiful she was. "I don't know, Jill. I had a couple of girlfriends at school, but I never spent too much time thinking about dating anyone seriously. I have stayed away from getting romantically involved with anyone; my work has always been my entire focus. I don't know what to say about what we just did; I can't put it into words. I always figured that sex would be just another biological function, something that had to be done to procreate the species, but with you, the word 'incredible' doesn't capture how I feel."

Smiling, she turned to him, reached down, and found that he was very aroused. "Can we try it again and see if we can find the right words? Would that be all right?"

"Oh, that would be more than all right." And like true scientists, they experimented again until they found the correct words.

*****

Their computer run at the Lawrence Livermore National Laboratory yielded the same results that they had at Pasadena. The fine-tweaking that the computer scientists had done with the project data reinforced to Murray and Jill that they were ready to present their findings to the National Academy of Science and The Griffith Group. Jill was amazed at the Blue Gene/P supercomputer system's computing power and told Murray, "We certainly have come a long way from the abacus and slide rule." After arriving back home in Pasadena, they were both surprised to find that instead of returning to the office right away; it was a Sunday afternoon after all; they made plans to do something together that evening. Jill was suddenly awakened to an awareness of her beauty and her sexuality, and she also discovered that she had an incredible appetite for lovemaking, something that Murray was more than happy to help her satisfy.

And with that, they discovered the joys of "romantic entanglements."

At her apartment that evening, lying in bed, she asked him, "Do you remember how you told me about your childhood? I sense that it might be painful to talk about it, but could you tell me?"

He thought for a second, and then slowly, he began talking about his life as a kid in West Texas.

Chapter Two

Twenty Years Earlier, West Texas

Oh, yeah, there should be no doubt about it; he'd show them, and he'd make them pay. This was young Murray's life goal. Hard to believe that there could be that much anger in a young boy, but it was there. And talk about hate, well, as they say out in West Texas, "I tell you *what*," this young man had enough hate for ten men. Out in West Texas, community was everything. Everyone took care of everyone else; that's just how it was. But the flip side was that everyone knew everyone else's business. And the local church, well, let me tell you, the local church was the center of everything.

His mother's name was RaeAnn, and as they used to say, she was quite a looker. RaeAnn had a job at the local diner one summer when she was still in high school and met Johnny, a good-looking, smooth-talking roughneck from Oklahoma. Old Johnny plied his considerable charm on that sweet young girl all summer long. Next thing you know, RaeAnn got herself all knocked up by Johnny. The only problem was that he decided not to stick around and abandoned his young girlfriend to fend for herself. Poor kid, she was just shy of her eighteenth birthday when young Murray drew his first breath out there in the Permian Basin. In their town, proper young women didn't associate with roughnecks, no, sir, much less come to know them in the Biblical sense. The small community that was her home since her birth and all of her friends and neighbors turned their collective backs on her. Those Bible-thumping hypocrites,

Murray would show them, he'd make them pay. They sit there and pray to some all-knowing, all-seeing Spirit who lives above the clouds. Well, there was no such thing. Any halfway intelligent person could figure that out. When his mother needed her family and friends the most, they avoided her and did their best to shun her, all the while spouting their nonsense of "Christian Charity." Make no mistake, he'd show them. He'd make them pay.

Murray had a pretty tough life growing up. His mother would have to work two to three jobs to support them. Then, after a long day at work, she'd go home to the run-down single-wide where she and Murray lived. When the young boy would come home from school each day, he would be there by himself until his mom came home from work. And any beauty that RaeAnn had was all but a faded memory by the time she was in her late twenties. But that wasn't the half of it: The stigma that his mother suffered was also visited upon him. Shunned and shamed by his classmates, he had no friends at school or in his trailer park. Even his mother's family avoided them, more bible thumping, more hypocrisy. How could a loving and benevolent Deity allow this to happen?

It finally began to dawn on him as to what was going on. As he was having breakfast in their trailer one morning, he looked up at his mother and asked, "Mom, how come Grandma and Grampa don't visit us?"

"Well, Sweetie," his mother replied, "they have a lot going on with all of their people from church, and that takes up a lot of their time."

"Can't we visit them in their church and meet all of their friends? I mean, we're here by ourselves all the time. When I come home from school, I'm by myself. When you come home from work, we're here by ourselves. Why can't we try to visit them at their church sometime? If we can't visit them at church because you're working, could we try to visit with them on Saturdays when they have those church get-togethers? Can we try that?"

Wearily, his mother looked at her boy and explained,

"You know that I work on most Sundays, and I'm so tired by the time the weekends roll around, I'm just beat, Baby. But I'll ask Grandma and Grampa if they can come by sometime to pick you up and take you to church with them someday. We'll see, OK?"

But she never did, or maybe she did ask, and good old Grandma and Grampa just gaffed her off. In his little heart of hearts, he knew. They didn't want anything to do with their own daughter or with their own grandson. It was all about their church and all about their church friends. It was all a big show for their all-powerful and all-loving God. How could this Deity's followers act in such a mean-spirited manner? To young Murray, there could only be one answer: there is no Supreme Being, there is no God, and there is no loving Jesus.

For what they did to his mom and him, he'd make them regret their belief in this pitiful little game. He'd make them regret that they spent their pathetic little lives chasing after a big crock, some big old pie in the sky.

Oh, yeah, he'd show them, he'd make them pay.

Thanks to those, as he called them, "bible-thumping morons," he had no friends. But just like the young Ebenezer Scrooge, he had his books. His books were his only friends. And he had the night sky. In the words of the old June Hershey and Don Swander song,

> The stars at night, are big and bright,
> deep in the heart of Texas!
> The prairie sky, is wide and high,
> deep in the heart of Texas!

He spent many lonely nights looking up at those big, bright stars in that wide, high Texas sky. Spurred on by his fascination with the night sky, he read everything he could about the stars, planets, planetary motion, and the expanding Universe. There were occasions out on the prairie when he could swear he could hear the Music of the Spheres. Good old Pythagoras. He knew what it was all about when he talked about the music of the spheres. He then learned about some of the giants of astronomy: Ptolemy, Copernicus, Galileo, Kepler, Hubble, and others. Digging even further, he was awakened to the mysteries of physics. How many twelve-year-old boys have read about Planck's constant and Einstein's various theories?

Throughout his early school years, Murray's teachers knew he was a very special young man, but the consensus was that he didn't apply himself. This all changed when he got into high school. Even though public schools in Texas had relatively high academic standards and were well-rated, his local schools could barely keep up with him. By the time he entered high school, he understood Max Planck's work and could confidently discuss Einstein's theory of relativity. He entered high school as a freshman, took his statewide academic exams and his test results were off the charts. Two months into his freshman year, he was promoted to the sophomore class, and his high school counselor had him take the Stanford-Binet test. His test score of 160 pegged him as a genius. By the Christmas break, he was ready to be transferred to the junior class. He completed his junior year and entered his senior year at fifteen. His counselors and mother decided that he should stay in high school for another year to help him mature, and at the age of sixteen, he graduated from high school. It was well known that Murray was on to much bigger and better things, but his classmates still shunned him. He endured two years of high school with no friends. He ate his lunch every day by himself—so much for Christian Charity.

MIT, Stanford, Cambridge, Caltech, the University of Chicago, and other institutions were all actively vying to get him into their schools. But where to go? He liked the story about Mr. and Mrs. Leland Stanford. If the stories were true, they were as rich as Croesus but still dressed and acted as if they, too, were from West Texas. Plus, the way that they honored their son reminded him of the relationship that he had with his mother.

Cambridge was the home of Sir Isaac Newton, Stephen Hawking, and Ernest Rutherford and had a rich history of groundbreaking research. The University of Chicago graduated

Edwin Hubble and Carl Sagan, and combined with all of the early work on nuclear energy that was accomplished there, this, too, was a very attractive option. CalTech had the JPL, plus it was in Southern California. But there was something about MIT that he liked. MIT may have been one of the most elite academic institutions in the world, but there was a little bit of West Texas whimsy mixed in with all of that academia. Any school that would acknowledge the beaver as "Nature's engineer" and would have "Tim the Beaver" as their mascot would be a fit with him, so with a full academic scholarship offered to him by MIT, it was to Cambridge, Massachusetts that young Murray decided to go.

Murray quickly discovered that his life would change significantly with his acceptance to MIT. Things had been fairly routine up to this point in his young life. His mother cared for almost everything he needed, including where he would lay his head down at night. But now, with his academic life beginning for him, he began to realize how easy things had been for him. One of the first things he had to do was apply for a place to live on campus at MIT. Interestingly enough, he found that he had to apply via a "lottery" for a place to reside at school. He learned that all incoming freshmen would be assigned temporary housing once they arrived in Cambridge. Still, he would have to enter the First-year housing lottery in May to be assigned a permanent residence on campus. Based on his research and reviews of the various dormitories, independent living groups, and fraternity houses, his first choice was to live at Baker House. He received word in June that his first choice was accepted.

Cambridge, Massachusetts
Mid-August

Cambridge, Massachusetts, was a far cry from West Texas, both geographically and culturally. He had never seen so much green grass and so many buildings, and this was just on the MIT campus. Plus, the way that these people talked! Everything and everyone moved so fast. Being from a small town in West Texas, most of the people he knew were regular old White folk. He knew many Hispanic and African-American folks, but to him, they weren't any different; they were just regular Texans, just like him. But in Massachusetts, he saw so many different people and heard so many different languages spoken. It was unbelievable, it was terrifying, but it was also exciting at the same time.

His orientation took place towards the end of August, and his initial exposure to his new collegiate life was overwhelming. His first stop was to check in for orientation at the Kresge Auditorium lobby.

Walking into the Kresge lobby, Murray was overwhelmed by the size of the hall. There was nothing this big back at his old high school; to be honest, there was nothing this big in his entire town. With his mouth agape and eyes scanning everything from the ceiling to the stage at the front of the room, he was in his own little world until someone bumped into him. "Come on, Rube, either get out of the way or grab a seat and sit the fuck down!" Shocked at being treated so rudely, he gathered his wits and apologized to his fellow student. He found the desk where he was supposed to check in for orientation. He was happy to discover that one of the first events for orientation was a barbecue scheduled at 5 PM that afternoon in Killian Court.

Murray found that the MIT barbecue was nothing like the barbecues they used to have back home. His mother would always bring him to her restaurant whenever they had a barbecue, but this allowed him to learn about MIT and see what his fellow students were like. He was always shy and reserved, and being exposed to all of these new people was a huge source of anxiety for him. The Dean for Student Life, Dr. Layos Szuperak, began to talk with the new incoming students, and this began to put him a bit at ease.

"Welcome to the Massachusetts Institute of Technology. I am Dean Layos Szuperak, and I have the privilege of being your Dean for Student Life. I wanted to give you all an introduction to life here at MIT and some background on our school, but first, I want to give you all a bit of help on how you can find your way around campus.

"First off, you may hear students and faculty talking about 'teaching 8.01' or 'meet me at 10-205.' This is not a secret code used to confuse everyone. It's just that we here at MIT do things a bit differently than other academic institutions. Let me expand on this: We do not refer to our courses of study by their traditional names. For example, we call mechanical engineering or physics by their respective 'course numbers.' To name a few of our programs, mechanical engineering is Course 2, physics is Course 8, and mathematics is Course 18. All of the subjects associated with that respective course are identified similarly. Here is one class that everyone will take here at MIT, 8.01. As you can see, since it begins with '8,' you know it is a physics subject. 8.01 is Physics I. Similarly, another course that you will become familiar with is 18.01, '18' means that it is a mathematics subject, 18.01 is Calculus. The mechanical engineering subject '2.05' is Thermodynamics and so on. Secondly, you will notice something like this in your subject listings: '8.01 in 26-152.' This means that Physics I will be held in classroom 26-152. Building 26 is also known as the Compton Labs, and 152 is on the first floor. We even call our buildings by their number. You all checked in for orientation in the lobby of the Kresge Auditorium. Kresge Auditorium is commonly called Building W16; the Maclaurin Building is called Building 10, and so on. You'll all catch on quickly. As a matter of fact, in about a year or so, someone may walk up to you and ask you how to get to the Maclaurin Building. You'll have no idea what they're talking about, you'll be puzzled for a second, and then you'll tell them they're looking for Building 10.

"I also wanted to point out that you will be meeting people from all over the world here at MIT, and because of that, you will appreciate learning things from different perspectives. Personally, my parents and my family fled Hungary in 1956 following the Hungarian uprising. We settled in Pennsylvania, and I went to school right here at MIT. You will find that many of your new classmates and your new friends will have interesting backgrounds and interesting family stories. You will learn as much from your fellow students as you will from your professors," Dr. Szuperak paused and then looked at his notes.

"Well damn, if you want to hear about an interesting family story, you should hear mine." He was so focused on the Dean's discussion that he didn't realize he was talking aloud. A young student standing beside Murray looked at him and said, "Excuse me?"

Murray looked over at a young Asian student and, with an embarrassed blush, replied, "Sorry about that; I should have kept my thoughts to myself. I'm just a bit nervous about being here."

"*You're* nervous? Let me tell you about being nervous. If I hadn't been accepted to MIT, my family would have disowned me. Talk about interesting families; you wouldn't believe the pressure I was under to get here." Offering his hand to Murray, he said, "I'm Brian Yang, from New York."

Murray looked down at Brian's outstretched hand, hesitated for a split second, and then reluctantly shook hands with Brian. "Murray Edgeton from West Texas. Sorry, Brian, I'm not used to being around so many people or in a place like this. I may as well be on Mars. And with the way I talk, every time I open my mouth, people out here look at me as if a mule had walked up to them and started talking. I figured it was better to keep my trap shut."

Brian thought about this and then offered, "Well, I imagine that at least you spoke English in your house. At home, everyone speaks Chinese. And I'm putting it lightly when I say they all 'speak' Chinese. Everyone at my house 'yells' at each other in Chinese. If you don't speak up and yell at my place, no one will hear you, so you'll find that I'm not too shy about speaking up. Stick with me, Murray, you'll catch on. What are you planning on studying here?"

"I'm interested in physics, or should I say Course 8. I've always been interested in why things do what they do, why the planets move through the sky at night, and why a tree falls down the way it does. How about you? What will you be studying here?" Murray asked.

"Computer Science," Brian answered. "I don't know what Course number it is, but I'm sure I'll find out." With that, Murray felt that he had met his first friend in Massachusetts.

By the weekend, his mother came out East to be with her son and help him transition from his hometown. She, too, was mesmerized by what she had seen; this trip to Massachusetts was only her second trip out of Texas in her lifetime. Before their trip to MIT, she and Murray spent one afternoon sitting at their small dining room table poring over maps and tourist guides of Boston. This city had so much history, and she was determined to take it all in. MIT had reserved a block of rooms for visiting parents and families, so on their first day in Cambridge, she and Murray crossed the Charles River and walked into the Grand City of Boston, Massachusetts. After two days of playing tourists, Murray bid a tearful goodbye to his mom, and his transition to being an MIT student began.

The Massachusetts Institute of Technology
Three months later

Murray was fortunate to have another Westerner as his roommate in Baker House, Anthony Martinez from Las Cruces, New Mexico. Anthony was a Mathematics major, Course 18 at MIT, whose father was an electrician at the White Sands Missile Range. Like Murray, Anthony was the first in his family to go to college, and at seventeen, he was also a youngster.

Unlike other institutions of higher learning, one would be hard-pressed to find much social activity occurring on the MIT campus between Sunday afternoons and Thursday evenings. The students did have a chance to go off campus for a quick dinner, but for the most part, they kept their proverbial noses to the grindstone during the week. During the week, their main chance to interact and visit each other was studying. Students were assigned problem sets in their classes, commonly called "p-sets," and they would meet in common areas, or in Murray's case, in Baker House's dining area, to work together on their p-sets.

Murray and Anthony were working on p-sets from their calculus class when Anthony said, "Come on, Murray, let's take a break. There is an ice cream shop right behind the school, maybe five or six blocks from here, right off First Street. It's called Toscanini's. It's supposed to have the best ice cream in the world. Let's head out and grab some before I start cursing Newton and Leibniz."

"Sure," answered Murray, "I tell you what, let's just finish this last problem, and then we'll go. Is that fair?"

"Yeah, that'll work."

About thirty minutes later, Murray and Anthony left Baker House and walked to Toscanini's. It was good to get away from studying for a bit, and like a lot of their talks, they found themselves talking about their homes.

"Murray, this is supposed to be good ice cream at Toscanini's, but I have to tell you, I miss my mom's cooking. You can't get anything out here that even resembles New Mexican food. You know about Hatch chilis, right?" Anthony asked.

"Yeah, we get them back home; I like them in my eggs in the morning. They're good in salsa, too."

Anthony continued, "Not only salsa, but how about in enchiladas? I like them early in the season when they're still green. My mom used to make the most incredible chili rellenos when the harvest began in August, but then she would also use them at the end of September when they're big and red. Man, do I miss eating some good food like that. All that these guys talk about out here is eating 'scrod,' what the hell is 'scrod?' I never heard of it until I got out here."

"I never heard of it either, but do you know Jim Wilson, one of those rich guys from Connecticut in Course 1? He told me he has a girlfriend who is an English major at Vassar. According to her, 'scrod' is the past pluperfect of 'screwed.' Can you believe these rich guys out here?" Murray asked.

"I know, and that one super wealthy guy from Long Island, what's his name? I can't remember, but he never even opens his mouth to talk. All you see are his teeth; he talks with his teeth clenched. Do you know who I'm talking about? He reminds me of that old rich guy from *Gilligan's Island*. What was his name? I can't remember, but I used to watch that show with my dad on that channel that plays old TV shows. But talking through your teeth like that, that must be something that the rich guys here in New England and New York do. Oh, here's Toscanini's."

The shop was filled with students, and there were no tables available, so they decided to get a couple of cones to go when one of the guys from a table full of upperclassmen called Murray over, "Yo, Murray, Anthony, come over and grab a seat."

Brage Galloway was a Course 12, planetary science major, who was another one of the students who came from a wealthy family in Connecticut. He lived in Baker House, about three doors down from Murray and Anthony. He was friendly enough, and Murray was happy to be recognized, something that had never happened back home. Sitting down, Murray and Anthony noticed that Brage had been drinking quite a bit and was pretty loaded. It looked like eating a bowl of ice cream after having a belly full of beer was the MIT thing to do.

Brage looked at his friends with a happy grin, "Hey guys, I'd like you to meet one of the brightest freshmen at MIT, my young friend Murray Edgeton. This guy knows more about universal gravitation than most of the guys in Course 12. Check this out. Imagine hearing about the gravitational force exerted by the Sun on a planet being proportional to the mass of the planet and inversely proportional to the square of its distance spoken with a West Texas hillbilly accent. It'll kill you!"

The guys at the table chuckled as Murray turned crimson. All that he could think at that moment was, *"hillbillies? Was Brage that stupid? Hillbillies don't come from West Texas. What a moron."* But very calmly, in his West Texas accent, Murray countered, "That's true enough, but I tell you *what*, recall that Newton's perturbation theory helped lead to the 1781 discovery of the seventh planet in our solar system, Uranus," he pronounced it with the correct inflection, 'YOOR a-nus.'

"Uranus' perturbations didn't behave quite as expected when Herschel discovered this planet, so other astronomers theorized that there must have been another planetary body not yet discovered that was influencing the motion of Uranus. This led to Johann Galle using Le Verrier's calculations to discover Neptune in 1846. So, while observing Uranus' strange perturbations led to an increase in knowledge, speaking out of Uranus," here he pronounced it 'your ANUS,' "doesn't help anyone."

There was dead silence. Other people were now listening to what was happening, and the whole place erupted with laughter. Someone yelled, "You tell him, Cowboy, glad that you put that rich boy Galloway in his place."

Brage looked at Murray through his beer-induced fog with new-found respect. While he didn't like being put down, he had to hand it to the kid, so to save himself some embarrassment, he jumped up, started patting Murray on the back, and yelled out, "Didn't I tell you, my buddy is the smartest kid at MIT!!" That was the first time that anyone called Murray "my buddy." He couldn't believe how good it made him feel. After that, Toscanini's was his favorite place in the world.

But something else became fully formed in Murray's psyche. While at MIT, he was introduced to the writings of Madalyn O'Hare, Richard Dawkins, and Christopher Hitchens. Their atheistic and anti-theistic writings had a significant impact on him. Then, he discovered some of the writings of Stephen Hawking. Hawking once wrote, "Because there is a law such as gravity, the universe can and will create itself from nothing. Spontaneous creation is the reason there is something rather than nothing, why the universe exists, and why we exist. It is not necessary to invoke God to light the blue touch paper and set the universe going." This is precisely how Murray felt. Everything boils down to empirical, observable, and testable science.

Since his youth, he had a significant distrust and distaste of "bible-thumpers," but since his time at MIT, where he was exposed to such clear thinking and an atmosphere that valued quantifiable and reproducible proof of observations, this distrust, this distaste metastasized into a deep anger of all things religious. The atheists simply believed that there is no Deity. The anti-theists, on the other hand, not only believed that there is no Deity, but they were also opposed to those who believed in God. What Murray had experienced in his young life and what he had learned in school made him not only oppose the "theists," but he also wanted to rub their noses into his deep-seated belief that "nobody was up there." Tortured by the fact that his mother, the only person in his life whom he loved, put all of her trust into an unreal Deity, he was determined to prove that there was no such thing as this Deity, a Deity who turned its back on his beloved mother, a Deity whose pitiful acolytes loaded them both down with the *ostraka* of the ancient Athenians and banished them from their miserable little town in West Texas. Fuck them, he'd make them pay, he'd show them.

Murray graduated from the Massachusetts Institute of Technology in three short years, and they awarded him his undergraduate degree in Physics. Three years later, at twenty-two, he was awarded his Ph.D. in Physics. He was invited to spend a year at MIT to do some additional research that he was working on. He looked forward to being able to investigate a theory that he had regarding Einstein's work on relativity.

During his doctoral studies, Murray found it fascinating that time travel was discussed in many ancient religious writings. In one of the early Hindu stories, the *Vishnu Purana,* King Raivata Kakudmi visits Heaven, where he meets Brahma, the Creator. When the king returns to Earth, he finds many years have passed, yet he has not aged. Several other Hindu and Buddhist stories discussed how time passes differently in Heaven than on Earth.

His thought was that the ancient writers could have observed that when they walked from their home to their temple in another city, it took them a considerable period of time, but when they rode their horses, the time to travel was much shorter. From this simple observation, they may have stumbled upon a primitive theory of time dilation. That was as good an explanation as any, but this became one of his guiding principles: "Keep things simple," echoing Einstein's quote, "make things as simple as possible, but no simpler." Murray's research was to take a simple approach to expand upon Einstein's theory of relativity and investigate the various geometries of Space-Time and motions in the Cosmos. Could understanding these geometries and motions lead to the ability to travel through time? Murray hoped to answer this and other questions, and this pursuit was the basis of his doctoral work.

Chapter Three

Washington, DC

"**Good morning, Dr. Edgeton, this** is your wake-up call. It is a beautiful fall day here in Northern Virginia, and our current temperature is a nice seventy degrees. We expect a high today of seventy-nine, but our humidity is a bit high at ninety percent. Is there anything that we can get for you this morning?"

Murray was staying at the Ritz Carlton in Tyson's Corner and mused aloud, "These folks certainly do it right. That wake-up call certainly beats the ringing phone and dial tone when you pick it up." He was here with several team members for a meeting with The National Academy of Science and The Griffith Group, looking for funding for his project. As Murray dressed for the morning conference, his thoughts returned, as they often did, to his old single-wide trailer back in West Texas. After seven years at MIT and three years at the Jet Propulsion Lab, he lost much of his Texas twang; his accent now was neutral. He could have been from Pierre, South Dakota, or Fresno, California, but the dust from the Permian Basin was part of his makeup and was in his blood. He came a long way from West Texas; if only his mother could see him now. She passed away shortly after he had completed his doctoral studies, and he knew that she had died from a broken heart. He had learned that his mother approached his grandmother, that old bat was still alive, and she had asked her if she could find it in her heart to go to Cambridge to witness Murray's hooding ceremony.

"Please, Mom, this is such an incredible honor, not only

for Murray but for our whole family. How many people from our town have graduated from college, much less graduating with a Ph.D. from MIT? It would be so wonderful if you could go out there with me and see what a beautiful town Cambridge is. We could go to Boston and visit all of those sites from the Revolutionary War. We could make a nice trip out of this for me and you. Please, Mom, please stop blaming Murray for what I did."

Her heartfelt plea fell on deaf ears as her mother said, "What you did was against God's Law and disgraced our whole family. Murray's high-falutin' schoolin' don't mean nothin'. Your sin is his sin. Don't you remember the passage when those Jews were going to crucify Jesus? All of those Jews yelled out, 'Let this sin be upon us and our children.' Why can't you see that your sin is his sin."

"But what about the forgiveness and mercy that Our Lord teaches us? Doesn't that include showing mercy and forgiveness to your own *grandson*?"

"No, it doesn't," the old lady shouted out. "Now get out of here. You have tried to use that bastard son of yours to get back at us. The only thing that I'm sorry about is that you're my daughter. We don't want to see you again. Now I already done told you, get out of here."

But that morning, as he looked at himself in the mirror as he was getting himself ready for his meeting, all that he could think about was that it wasn't only that old hag of a grandmother that killed his mom, it was Grandmother's belief in that Church of hers. Those church people had just as much to do with his mother's death as did that cerebral hemorrhage; "apoplexy," as those morons back home called it. Nope, those bible-thumpers, those hypocrites, they did it. "Oh, yeah," he said to himself, "won't they be surprised when science can evict their Deity from this world of ours? We'll be much better for it."

His anti-theistic attitude and his earlier anger of all things religious had metamorphosized into a complete loathing and hatred of not simply all things spiritual. He began to hate and loathe all of those who believed in God. This hatred and loathing became the prime mover in his life and his life's work.

*****

    Murray was surprised to see several representatives from the Department of Defense and the Department of Energy at the meeting, in addition to the team from the National Academy of Science and The Griffith Group. Murray hoped that The Griffith Group, a private industrial and research firm that offered to fund various research projects, could come through for him. Griffith's funding would allow him to pursue his project without the bureaucratic strings attached that would come with government funding. The presence of the Defense and Energy Departments' representatives at the meeting confirmed his suspicions of those strings. Still, he needed the funding, so this meeting was crucial to the project's success.

    Murray was introduced to the group and started the team's presentation. "Good morning. Thank you all for your time this morning. In the interest of time, I'd like to jump right into our presentation this morning regarding our project and follow up with a Q&A period. At the Jet Propulsion Laboratory, we have been involved in some ground-breaking research into the Space-Time Continuum. This work has expanded on the work of Albert Einstein, specifically his General Theory of Relativity. We have established a team of physicists, astronomers, engineers, and mathematicians, and informally, our project has become known as "The Einstein Project."

    "For those of you who may not be familiar with Professor Einstein and his work, he lived from 1879 to 1955 and essentially rewrote what the world knew to be the laws of Nature. His work in the early twentieth century forever changed all that the world knew regarding space, time, light, and gravity. Einstein's work led him to conclude that space and time are not separate and distinct phenomena but inextricably linked into a single phenomenon. This phenomenon is what we now call the space-time continuum. He postulated that the space-time continuum has our physical dimensions of length, width, and height combined with the fourth dimension, time."

"Dr. Edgeton?" One of the representatives from The Griffith Group interrupted Murray's presentation with a question. "My background as an attorney is in law, not physics, and I'm a bit confused about this 'continuum,' can you explain this in terms that even a lawyer could understand? Maybe something akin to a junior high school science class." This got a few chuckles from the audience.

Smiling, Murray continued. "Certainly, that's a good question. Thank you for bringing it up. Physicists explain the space-time continuum as a large sheet of fabric. Let me try to illustrate this: Think of a huge metal sheet, like a large section of a Cyclone fence, held up by four enormous support pillars. Now, take a large object, for example, a large metal wrecking ball, and place this ball in the middle of our large metal sheet. This wrecking ball will cause a large "dip" in the metal sheet. This large dip represents a distortion in our sheet, a distortion in the space-time continuum. Einstein discusses this distortion in one of his most famous theories, what I mentioned earlier, the General Theory of Relativity. In this theory, Einstein demonstrated that *matter,* our large wrecking ball, causes the space-time continuum, our metal sheet, to curve. This curve, this distortion in our space-time continuum, is what Einstein concludes gives rise to what we call 'gravity.' He also demonstrated that a path of light will follow the gravitational curve of space and that time will move slower when the gravitational forces are powerful. Does that explain the concept to you?"

"Yes, I think it does. Thank you, Dr. Edgeton."

"Thank you, sir. Now, here is where this gets interesting. In theory, and I have to emphasize this, *in theory*, astrophysical phenomena or cosmic events could distort the space-time continuum to such a degree that the space-time continuum could form a loop onto itself. This loop, known as the closed-timelike curve, could form a portal into the past. Additionally, another hypothetical structure called 'a wormhole,' described as a hole in the space-time fabric that could connect different times and places within the space-time continuum."

The attorney from The Griffith Group jumped in again, "Dr. Edgeton, please excuse my interruption, but my brain is beginning to ache trying to wrap my head around what you're saying. Are you saying that due to these astrophysical phenomena, time travel is possible? In theory, that is."

"Thank you again for your question. Might I ask, what is your name, please?"

"David Bianchi, but please call me Dave."

"Thanks, Dave," answered Murray. "Yes, that is exactly what our research and Einstein's theory show. Recall what Einstein concluded: if the gravitational forces are very strong, the fourth dimension in the space-time continuum, which is to say, 'time,' will behave very differently. Einstein postulated that it would slow down, but could it display other behaviors? That's one of the other areas that we're researching. Secondly, and I don't mean to repeat myself, I need to make this point crystal clear: A further distortion in the space-time continuum could give rise to the phenomenon called the 'closed-timelike curve,' which could form a portal to the past. Combined with that, 'wormholes' can connect different times and places in the continuum.

"Think of it this way: no, let me back up. The conventional way to think of 'time' is that it is a linear process. To illustrate this, we know that the Roman Empire, if you include the Roman Kingdom, the Roman Republic, and then the Roman Empire, lasted roughly 1,000 years, starting around the sixth century before the common era and ending around the fourth century of the common era. I'm not completely sure of the dates, but you get the idea. We look at 'time' as something that marches in a linear fashion, and then it is gone, but Einstein said that 'time' is not linear; it is part of a continuum. Look at our example of the large cyclone fence representing our space-time continuum. Imagine that we have a giant stethoscope that can be used to 'listen' to different parts of our continuum. We can use the stethoscope to 'plug in' to different spots in time; that's a wormhole; it connects different times and places in the continuum and could be considered an 'access point' to the space-time continuum. The other connection I mentioned is the closed-timelike curve, where the space-time continuum folds back on itself and offers another access point.

"What we would like to report to you is that through our research, experimentation, and computer modeling and simulations, we believe that we are on the cusp of determining and predicting the behavior of closed-timelike curves and wormholes. We are fairly confident that we can access these phenomena and actually travel through time."

The room was incredibly quiet; you could have heard a pin drop. To say that his announcement was mind-boggling would be an understatement. Finally, Attorney Dave Bianchi broke the silence and asked two straightforward questions, "Dr. Edgeton, why would you want to do this? To what end would traveling through time serve?"

"Dave, and to all of you in this room, that is the question that must be asked. Why would we, as a people, do something like this? We could cite any number of reasons why we should do this. We would be unlocking the secrets of the Universe or proving Einstein's theory. But in the final analysis, why should we do this? This is the same question asked in the late 1950s when we were embarking on the space race with the Soviet Union: why should we go to space? We could talk about all of the commercial benefits that have come out of our space program, for example, GPS, personal computers, and so many others, but why, indeed, did we go into space? Then, after we answer that, let's ask the next question: why should we embark on this project? I think that it's because we're humans. A history review has shown that we question things and need to find answers to things. As a species, we have been doing this for our entire existence. Think of those who sailed across uncharted oceans or crossed the land bridge from Siberia to the New World. We have to do these things."

The group debated this for hours. In the end, Dr. Edgeton and the Einstein Project got their funding.

Chapter Four

It had been six months since the meeting in Washington, DC, and the Einstein Project team had made considerable progress in their work. With the infusion of funds, they were able to contract a computer modeling and simulation team under the direction of Jill McAllister. They were tasked to develop the appropriate algorithms and mathematical equations needed to explain the behavior of the space-time continuum and to perform the simulations of their models. One of the major findings that came out of their research was the correlation between astronomical phenomena occurring in space and unexplained astronomical events occurring on Earth. The team spent a significant amount of time and effort investigating these phenomena.

Jill walked into Murray's office, where he and Nate were modifying the team's schedule; she appeared to be extremely excited. "Good afternoon, gents. As you asked, I have the results of our latest run, I think that you two need to see them."

"I'm sorry, Jill," Nate replied, "I've been stuck in my office for the last few days and have been a bit out of the loop, was this the aurorae run that you just completed? I've been hearing a lot about this."

"Yes, Nate, we had the opportunity to search through archival records looking for unusual astronomical activity for the past few millennia. You would be amazed at some of the records that some of those astronomers kept. Even the astronomers from the times of antiquity. Unbelievable."

"Jill, let's take a look. Nate and I have been waiting to see these results," Murray chimed in; he was also extremely excited.

"Thanks," Jill gave an impish smile and a raised eyebrow to him who flashed a quick wink to her in reply. Their relationship had gotten very serious, but they were very discreet. "Let me start off by talking about events that occurred well in the past. As I was saying, some of the ancient astronomers and their schools kept meticulous records of their observations and their calculations. We always talk about Tycho Brahe, Galileo, and Copernicus as being 'early astronomers' and they were, but their work was in the 1500s. There are ancient astronomers who studied the Cosmos and described accurately various astronomical phenomena over three thousand years ago. Around 900 B.C. Egyptian astronomers developed a calendar that had 365 days. They based this upon observations of Sirius and correlated its cycle with the annual flooding of the Nile. These guys were well ahead of their time. Then we had the Mesopotamian astronomer Naburimannu, who, in the 5th century B.C., calculated accurately the lunar cycle to be 29.5306 days. That's pretty exact for work that was done 2,500 years ago. These astronomers and others, Arybhata of India, Aristarchus of Samos, and Hipparchus of Nicaea, all had schools of astronomy established and they performed some amazing research.

"We had the opportunity to analyze their archival records and were able to plot their data of unexplained astrophysical phenomena. For example, we looked at unexplained eclipses or aurora-type activity in areas where we would not expect to see aurorae, either Aurora Borealis or Aurora Australis. Aurorae are also normally seen at what is called magnetic midnight, and what we had seen reported in all of these observations was that the aurorae were observed on some occasions before dawn or, in most instances, during the daytime. The astronomy folks we talked with said that that is extremely unusual, almost unheard of, and interesting to say the least.

"They were able to plot these phenomena and develop a mathematical model from them." She sat down at the table with her colleagues and opened up her printout. "As you can see, we have data going back to 650 B.C. from various Mesopotamian, Egyptian, Persian, and Indian schools. The modeling and simulation team has subjected these data to a number of tests and it looks like these strange phenomena have been occurring in the Eastern Mediterranean area and the Middle East with some regularity for the past three thousand years. With further modeling, the team feels that they might actually be able to predict when the next aurora-like event will occur.

"But what's even more exciting is what the Astronomy section found. Something unusual has been reported in astronomical literature and they did a search of all of the astronomy records for the past several hundred years. In the 1600's some contemporaries of Galileo, Kepler, and Huygens reported seeing what they called a 'blink' in the Cosmos. Then, in 1870, one of the priest astronomers working for Father Angelo Secchi at the Roman College Observatory, I think that was the forerunner of the Vatican Observatory, observed what he called 'an accordion closing in space.' By the time the 1900s rolled around, sophisticated cameras were taking photographs of the Cosmos; they actually recorded this 'accordion fold.' Astrophysicists called this a 'slight contraction.'

"Here is where this gets *really* exciting. The team ran the numbers and it appears that whenever this 'contraction' in space was observed, the unexplained aurora occurred on Earth at the same time. They have done significant modeling on this and it appears with significant certainty that these two events are related."

"What are you saying?" Murray asked. He was very controlled, but he felt that his breakthrough was about to happen.

"Remember how the Einstein-Rosen wormhole is described, a tunnel that connects two separate points in space-time. This could be different locations, different points in time, or both. What the team is thinking is that this accordion fold, this contraction in the Cosmos is the closed-timelike curve, and the unexplained aurorae are the wormhole connecting two separate chronological and geographical points in space-time. We think that we have found the portal into the space-time continuum."

*****

Further research was done by the Einstein Project team, and what was discovered was that the closed-timelike curve and the associated aurora activity were not random; they occurred with predictable regularity. These occurrences of both phenomena were plotted and analyzed and they found that when they did occur, they could be associated with a specific geographical point on Earth. They coined the term "Time Launch Points," or "TLP's" to describe the intersection of the closed-timelike curve, the wormhole, and the geographical location. The TLP is where they planned on accessing the space-time continuum. Murray had received the latest results from the computer modeling and simulation team and he was discussing these results with Nate.

"Nate, looking at this latest simulation, it appears as if we had significant TLP activity in the Mideast in the early part of the First Century of the Common Era, right around the year 33. If the data are correct, it also looks as if we have experienced additional TLPs in recent times. Jill told me this morning that her team is running simulations right now and they're predicting that we will have another TLP occurring in the very near future. Her team also pointed out that it appears that the TLP will be associated with an area in the Middle East, looks like present-day Israel."

Nate sat there with his hands steepled. "Murray, you know what this means. If we can identify where and when the next TLP will occur, we may have the ability to access the continuum. We have the chance to prove Einstein right."

"Damn, Nate, not only that, but we have the chance to

demonstrate that time travel is possible! I knew it. I told you that we were going to do this!" He stood up and walked around the room for a moment to collect his thoughts. "Let's get some of the team members together. We have some planning to get to, what do you think?"

"Absolutely. I think that since we're fairly certain that we can access the continuum, now that all of the theorizing is complete, we need to spell out what we're going to do. What's our objective? Who or what are we going to send into the continuum? If we're going to send a human subject, will we be able to get the person back? Lots of things to discuss. I don't know about you, but I'm a bit overwhelmed by all of this. What are some of the discoveries or inventions that forever changed mankind? Agriculture? The invention of the wheel? Gunpowder? What we're doing is as important as those breakthroughs, if not more important. This is something that can change the trajectory of our species. This is very heady stuff; I'm getting a bit apprehensive."

"No, shit, Nate. This is how the Wright Brothers must have felt, or Tesla, or Lister. For any of those people who made a huge impact on our world, they probably all voiced the same concern as you. No, we're doing the right thing. Let's go ahead and get a group together to come up with our objectives to guide us through this next phase, sound good?"

"Sounds good to me. Let me make a suggestion, why don't we get Jay, PK, and Mo together with me, you, and Jill to put some objectives together. Maybe a smaller group might be easier to work with, just my thoughts."

"Yeah, that sounds good, could you put this together? I will be available for any date and time that you can get these folks corralled up. Damn, I'm getting excited!"

"Of course, my friend, this is the culmination of your life's work, I'm very excited for you. I'll send out invites for you."

The group met the following day to develop objectives for the Einstein Project. The newly assigned members were Dr. Morris "Mo" Kimber, head of the Astronomy team, physicist

Dr. Jay Agrawal and astrophysicist Dr. P.K. Chakraborty.

Murray opened the meeting. "Thank you all for taking time out of your schedules today. As was discussed in Nate's invite to you all and as the entire Einstein Project team is talking about, Jill's group has made the breakthrough that we have all been working so hard to achieve. Time travel is a very distinct possibility, and we believe that we know how to make this happen. But before we proceed any further, we need to establish a workable and achievable set of objectives to guide our efforts moving forward. Let me open this up, what do you all think?"

Jay Agrawal asked, "Murray, as a physicist, working on this project has been a fulfillment of my life's work and I am very happy to be involved with this—"

"I hear a 'but' coming."

"You're right. We're here to develop some objectives, and that's fine. Objectives let us know 'what' we're doing, but I think the bigger question is 'why are we doing this.' Can we answer this question first? I'd like us to have on record something like a vision or mission statement, why we're doing what we're doing. Can we publish something similar to what you all said back in D.C.?"

Nate replied to the question, "Let me jump in really quickly. Jay, I'm glad that you brought up what we said back in D.C. Murray gave a good answer, we're unraveling the secrets of the universe, and we're verifying Einstein's theory. Those are good reasons to do what we're doing but go back to the basics. What do we, as scientists and physicists, do? What is our main goal in physics? We try to understand why the universe behaves in the way that it does. Isn't that correct? If it is, I think that we have answered the question. We're physicists, scientists; this is what we do."

His answer got heads nodding and smiles all around the table. Mo Kimber then said, "I agree with that; that is what we do. As for objectives, we need to look at a number of things. First off, if we can access the space-time continuum and send something or someone through time, how do we get them back? Secondly, how can we objectively and quantifiably demonstrate that we were successful? What will be our measure of success? Thirdly, if we have to send a fellow human, whom are we going to send? Another thing to think about is, where will we send our time traveler and what time period will they be going to?"

The discussion continued in this vein for some time with all of the participants voicing similar questions and concerns. At the end of the meeting, the team had a fairly good idea of what their objectives would be. Their first objective would be to demonstrate with a very high statistical probability that time travel is possible through the Time Launch Portal. This could be accomplished by their modeling and experimentation. The second objective would be to determine how a "time traveler" would be returned to the present time. Their third objective would be to determine "what success looks like." In addition to the safe return of the time traveler, the collection and return of artifacts were given as another tangible measure of success. If the collection of an artifact was to be a measure of success, it was apparent that a human would have to be sent through the portal. This led to the fourth objective: Who would be selected to go collect this artifact? Fifth, they had to determine when the next TLP was going to "open." And last, it had to be determined to what time period and to what geographical location the time traveler would be transported.

The following week P.K. Chakraborty met with Mo Kimber to discuss his latest findings. "Mo, I think that I'm on to something regarding our Time Launch Portal. Right after Jill and I completed our work on the contraction, I thought that I saw something in the model. I've been running these calculations over and over for the past ten days or so, I think that I'm right about this."

"Show me what you've got, P.K."

He pulled out his laptop and ran a simulation. "I put this together based on the final model that we had, we can go over the hard data later, but look at this simulation. The behavior of the TLP shows that the cycle is predictable. See how the flux moves in this orientation and then how it reverts back to this baseline? When I was looking at the simulation at normal speed, I missed it, but when I sped it up, here, take a look." He ran the simulation fast-forward, and the TLP's behavior moved in a cyclic fashion. "It looks to me as if the TLP is behaving in, for lack of a better term, a 'delivery and return method.' Look at the intersectionality of all three elements: the closed-timelike curve, the wormhole, and the geographical location. There, see that? Now look at it right here. It returns to the same locus. We'll continue to run this, but I'm fairly certain that we can insert an object, or a subject, into the TLP right here," he pointed to the initial point in the simulation which represented the access point into the TLP. "Then the transport takes place to here," he pointed to the second point in the simulation which showed the destination back in time, "and then the return back to the initial access point, here. We have a lot of work to do on this, Mo, but we can safely say that we can access the space-time continuum at the Time Launch Portal, transport something or someone back into time, and then safely return our object or subject home. I'll need more time to get us to a higher degree of certainty, but I think we've got it. What do you think?"

Mo nodded, "Let's get together with Murray and Nate. Great job to you and your guys. I think that you're right."

*****

By the following Spring, the Einstein Project team was able to identify with a high degree of certainty when and where TLPs would open for the "delivery" into the space-time continuum, and through sophisticated modeling, they could forecast when they were going to reopen for the "return" back to the present time. It appeared as if they could now test their time travel theory by inserting a human subject into the TLP and returning the subject home. It became apparent to them what this meant—they could travel through time, and because of that, they had the potential to alter events from the past. Membership of the Einstein Project had grown to include ethicists and philosophers at this time, and the debate began about the ramifications of altering past events. It became evident that altered events could have far-reaching and potentially very negative consequences, so the decision was made that if time travel became a reality, a team could travel to a point in the past, but their mission would be to observe only and not attempt in any way to alter any past events.

Chapter Five

As the research continued into the possibility of a human subject being able to travel through time through the TLP, the discussion of what *type* of person could be selected to participate in this new program was undertaken.

One of Mo Kimber's retired professors, Dr. Kenneth Eustis, worked with the fledgling National Aeronautics and Space Administration, NASA, during the late 1950s, and he was brought in as a consultant to discuss their selection process of the Project Mercury astronauts.

Dr. Eustis was in his late 80s and looked as if he could still run marathons, which he did until his 60s. "You know, when we embarked on Project Mercury back in the 50s, we were all in a state of, how can I describe this, we were all in a state of 'optimistic disbelief.' Understand that our task was to put a man into Earth's orbit and then return him home safely. No one had ever done this; we had no template to work with or experience, and we were truly flying by the seat of our pants. It was all very exciting; we were stepping into the unknown.

"Here we had this huge task, 'put a man into space and bring him back home safely.' That was the key. We were discussing 'manned' space flight. What kind of man would we put into space? What were the criteria for selection? So, what does a big governmental agency do when faced with a question or a problem? You form a task force. But we were lucky. We had some great guys back then, smart, dedicated, and no messing around—top-notch engineers who wanted to get things done. NASA formed the Space Task Group, the STG. We were tasked to manage America's manned spaceflight program, and one of our first projects was to develop criteria for selecting spaceflight candidates. Yeah, we had some great folks on our teams back then. Our boss was Bob Gilruth, the Golden Gopher from Duluth—a brilliant engineer and manager. Then, talk about a great group of guys; guess who else we had on our team? Chris Kraft. Does anyone here besides Mo know what Chris' full name was? Christopher Columbus Kraft, how's that for an auspicious beginning for a team involved with space exploration? Yeah, we had a great bunch of guys."

"Dr. Eustis, tell them about the computers you all had back then," piped up his old student.

"Oh, yes, our computers. We had eight women on our team, and their title was 'computers,' which refers to the original definition of the word 'one who computes.' They ran all of our calculations on adding machines. Can you believe that? We were putting together a plan to send men into space and doing our calculations on those old mechanical tabulating machines; as I said, we just got things done.

"Going back to our task of candidate selection. We developed a checklist of traits each of our candidates should have. The ideal candidate would have to be able to function in an extremely high-stress environment, make critical decisions with limited information, and be in top physical condition. What kind of people fit into that category? You could look at airplane pilots, submarine officers, or deep-sea divers. We could choose from a large pool of candidates, but we decided to simplify this process and focus on military test pilots as our primary source of candidates. Plus, we had to consider that our military test pilots were all military officers, and as such, they all had security clearances. Being involved with the space program required handling highly classified information, so we solved one of our problems right there."

"Dr. Eustis," Nate asked. "I can see some parallels

between what you did in the 1950s and what we are trying to accomplish here with the Einstein Project. But what you said regarding using your team members to perform all of your calculations on those analog devices, can you go over that again, please?"

"Calling them analog devices is very generous, Dr. Joseph. A lot of the work that our very bright 'computers' did was with a good old pencil and paper. There were some very bright and dedicated women in our group, and we were fortunate to have them working with us. We had three mathematicians who happened to be African-American and had to deal with a lot of the nonsense we had to deal with back then. They took all of our data and validated them by hand. Think\ of how brilliant these women were!"

"I can only imagine, Dr. Eustis," Nate continued. "But how could you all 'test' a lot of the systems that were going to be flying into space? You didn't do any modeling or computer simulations back then, right?"

"That's a great question, Dr. Joseph. No, we couldn't do the types of modeling and simulation that you all can do now. When those astronauts, and the Soviet cosmonauts, too, for that matter, went into space, the predictions of the performance of their equipment were based, for the most part, on pure theory. Aerospace engineers, mechanical engineers, structural engineers, and metallurgical engineers, we all put our heads together and worked things out on paper or with a slide rule. Think about it, what do Ptolemy, Euclid, Archimedes, the Roman Engineers, Einstein, Bohr, and Hawking all have in common? The language of mathematics. The numbers don't lie. We demonstrated that with the Mercury Program."

Dr. Eustis' talk lasted another hour, and the Einstein Project team learned much from his successful and practical experience with Project Mercury. Murray decided to mirror, to a degree, the approach taken by Dr. Eustis and NASA in selecting candidates as potential subjects for the Einstein Project. NASA devised an initial selection process focused on various physical, professional, and psychological criteria. The

Einstein Project's criteria would not be too different. All of the Mercury 7 astronauts were military test pilots and understood the dangers inherent to their missions. The Einstein Project's candidates would also have to be fully aware and accepting of the risks of their potential mission. Similar to NASA's STG, the members of the Einstein Project began to develop a list of criteria for their candidates, and like NASA, they adopted a name for their candidates. In the late 1950s and early 1960s, both the American and the Soviet space programs coined names for their space travelers: The Soviets used the name "Cosmonaut" from the Greek meaning "sailor of the universe," and the Americans used the name "Astronaut" meaning "sailor of the stars." The Einstein Project team coined the term "Krononauts," Greek for "sailor through time" for their candidates. They didn't know if this name would "stick," but they decided to use it as a placeholder for the time being.

Candidate Selection Group Meeting

"I don't know, Murray, 'Krononaut' sounds like some kind of pastry, maybe a doughnut. I prefer calling them 'Argonauts,' as Jason and his sailors faced dangers unknown to the Ancient Greeks, just like our guys. 'Krononauts' sounds hokey. We have to come up with something better than that," Nate said as they prepared for a meeting with the rest of the team.

Murray replied, "Yeah, whatever. We can look at calling these guys something else later on. What we need to do now is determine the criteria for team selection. I liked what NASA's STG did in the late '50s; they simplified their process by using the most logical candidates available. Remember the old maxim, 'The simplest explanation is probably the best one?' What was that, Ockham's Razor?"

Dr. Joseph laughed at his reply. "Remember that William of Ockham was a Franciscan Friar. He was a scholar and theologian who attributed this preference for simplicity to 'defend the idea of divine miracles.' His correct phrase was 'entities should not be multiplied beyond necessity.' Even when Einstein was unlocking the universe's secrets, he stated something similar to Friar William. I'll make a believer out of you yet."

"Fuck that, Nate, that will never happen," quipped Murray as he was organizing his papers. "By the way, how could you quote that guy so quickly?"

"The Franciscans trained me for twelve years; you can't beat them for blending academics with humility and respect for God. The Franciscans focus on doing 'the good' and using common sense. The Friars are so much better than the Jesuits regarding their pragmatic approach to things. I shudder thinking about being taught by the Jesuits, but I think you'd probably love them."

"That's bullshit, and you know it. The Jesuits are probably the only people among you deluded believers who have any brains. I met one of them at a symposium back at MIT. He was on the Vatican Observatory staff, and he returned to the States for that conference. He was brilliant but a very strange guy. All right, let's head in and meet with the rest of the guys to get this show on the road."

Nate grinned and shook his head at his friend as they walked down the hallway to the conference room to meet with the team. In the conference room, the project team was already assembled. They were all standing around the refreshment table, stuffing their faces with pastries, hot tea, and coffee, and all conversation stopped when Murray and Nate walked into the room. The team members, all very accomplished and brilliant in their respective fields, were to an individual intimidated by Dr. Edgeton. It wasn't that he was a bully or a driven taskmaster; it was because of his sheer brilliance that people were always on edge around him. He did not suffer fools very well, and no one in the group wanted to be on his "bad side." He couldn't understand why people were not as driven as he was, and the least he expected of them was that they came prepared for his meetings. There were too many instances of his shredding subordinates to pieces if they gave a poorly prepared briefing.

There was a large wooden conference table in the middle of the room, and it looked as if a small section of the rainforest had been used to construct it. Murray rushed into the room and, without preamble, barked, "OK, let's get started." Everyone hustled to get to their seats.

The project team members seated around this table could have been a brain trust for almost any nation on Earth. Their numbers included some of the brightest engineers at NASA: theoretical physicists from academia, ethicists and philosophers from Harvard's Edmond J. Safra Center for Ethics and from The Hastings Center, and rounding out the team were physicians, psychologists, and human performance specialists.

Murray jumped right in to open the discussion. "We have been working on the Einstein Project for quite some time. Our theoretical research and experimentation have been completed or are nearing completion, and we're still way behind our initial timeline projection. Dr. Joseph and I were under the impression that following our initial meetings, a preliminary list of criteria for candidate selection was to be completed by now. Has our group finalized these criteria?"

"We have, Dr. Edgeton," answered Arne Johansson, one of the NASA engineers on the team and the informal project leader of the selection group. "What we wanted to do this morning was to present our selection criteria to you and Dr. Joseph and then offer you gentlemen the opportunity to weigh in on our findings. Hopefully, we can finalize them this morning."

Looking at Murray, Nate said, "Thank you, Arne, that sounds good. Why don't you let us know how you developed your criteria and arrived at your results."

"Thank you, Nate. Our group continued in the direction we had initially taken, that is, to mirror to a degree the work that NASA did when developing the criteria for the Mercury Seven astronauts. As you may recall, NASA's STG had a relatively simple list of criteria for astronaut selection. They wanted candidates who were in excellent physical condition and within a certain height and weight limit due to the spatial constraints of the Mercury Space Capsule. They then had to meet a very specific, mission-related component as they had to be a qualified jet pilot, a test pilot school graduate, and have at least 1,500 hours of flight time. They also needed to find a group that understood the secret nature of military missions and could be trusted not to disclose that confidence. Military pilots were determined to meet all of these criteria, and narrowing the field to military pilots streamlined the entire process.

"Lastly, test pilots and jet pilots know that their jobs are inherently dangerous, but the dangers are known. For the Mercury program, these pilots would fly into Earth's orbit. They were flying into space. They understood that flying into space, as in any flight, your vehicle could fail. Again, the dangers are *known*. But in our situation, this wouldn't be simply a 'Space Program,' but a 'Space-Time Program.' We have no idea what all of the dangers might be. What kind of person would take that risk? Allow me to turn this part of our discussion over to Dr. Oliphant. Steve, please take it from here."

Dr. Stephen Oliphant was the psychiatrist on the team, and he collaborated with the psychologists and other members to address the psychological aspect of the prospective candidates. Arne selected Dr. Oliphant to represent the team and present their findings for today's meeting.

"Thank you, Arne. Gentlemen, our group utilized criteria similar to those employed by NASA. For example, we had to consider the 'mission critical' criteria and the individual factors. As Arne stated, what kind of person would risk facing unknown dangers?

"Let's consider the 'mission critical' criteria first. Our experiments and theorizing have shown that the possible travel through a wormhole will be more physically demanding than anything a human has experienced in our history. Therefore, our first criterion would be that our Krononaut would have to be a highly conditioned individual, more physically fit than most of us can imagine, and also very mentally tough."

"Let me ask a quick question," interjected Murray. "Steve, Arne, what do you think of that name, Krononaut? I know we bantered that name around for a while, but this is the first time I have heard it used in a formal setting. What do you all think?"

"Well," answered Steve, "it is an interesting name and follows along with what the US and USSR did with their space programs."

Arne chimed in next. "I don't know if I like it. A quick story: I used to watch those old classic fantasy movies on Saturday morning TV when I was a kid. I could watch 'Jason and the Argonauts' all the time. Do you remember that stop-motion animation used when Jason was fighting those skeletons? The Argonauts, now those guys were adventurous warriors, but when I hear 'Krononauts?' It doesn't resonate with me. A 'Krononaut' doesn't sound like an adventurous warrior. "

"That's what Nate was saying earlier. He said we should call them Argonauts as they're sailing into unknown waters," Murray said. "I don't want to sound as if I'm waffling; I agree with what Steve was saying; it does follow what we did with the space program, but I also agree with Mr. Johansson; the name doesn't resonate with me either."

"Let's look at this from another perspective," suggested Nate. "Why did the US call their space travelers 'astronauts' and the USSR called theirs 'cosmonauts?' Because they had to give the public a name of these heroes. With the Einstein Project, this will be completely shrouded in secrecy, correct? The public shouldn't know about this for some time, so why do we even have to give a name to our team members? Do they need to be given a name?"

There appeared to be assent with the group, and Murray answered, "That's what I was thinking. Thanks, Nate, and to be honest, gentlemen, I hate that fucking name."

"Thank you, Murray," Steve said, "I guess that clears it up, but as we're all being honest here, I'd prefer to talk about 'Jason and the Argonauts.'"

This entire group laughed at this. Steve was known for not having much of a sense of humor, and his unexpected quip relieved some of the tension in the room.

Waiting for the laughter to die down and with his face blushing a bit, he continued, "In addition to being in top physical and mental condition, our candidate must have the ability to carry out and complete a mission in which the extent of the dangers associated with this mission are unknown. The candidate must also be able to operate in a harsh desert environment and possess significant survival skills. The candidate will also need combat skills, as the potential for hostilities might be a factor. Team members must also have mechanical skills, linguistic capabilities, and a high-security clearance. Lastly, the data indicate that the TLP will open in present-day Israel. As the area in which the team will be operating will be ancient Palestine and Judea, our team members must have the physical appearance of an individual from the Middle East or the Mediterranean area as they must blend in with the locals, as it were.

"Just as NASA decided to narrow their search by focusing on military pilots, we feel we can also narrow our search. Our group listed our candidate's requirements by asking: What kind of individual possesses the following skill set?" He passed a folder to each of the attendees. "Looking at the handout in front of you, here are the main requirements for our candidates," the requirements on the handout were as follows:

1- Top physical condition.
2- Mental toughness and the physical courage to deal with unknown dangers.
3- Combat skills.
4- The ability to operate in harsh environments.
5- Significant survival skills.
6- The ability to utilize the terrain for concealment.
7- The ability to evade capture by a hostile force.
8- Mechanical skills.
9- High-security clearance.
10- Language skills.

Steve continued, "NASA narrowed their search by focusing on military pilots. Looking at our skill set, it became obvious that our search could be narrowed down very quickly by focusing on our military special forces and special operations teams, for example, the elite Navy SEALs, Army Delta Force, Marine Corps Force Reconnaissance, and Air Force PJ teams. Research into these elite groups, they call themselves 'operators,' also shows that they can operate and adapt very well to rapidly changing conditions and when the level of danger escalates quickly. Anecdotally, it has been said that these operators relish doing dangerous tasks, such as high altitude, low opening parachute jumps, and swimming long distances in the ocean at night. We feel that selecting candidates from these elite groups will provide us with a team that will have the greatest chance of completing and surviving this program. I want to open this up to any questions you may have or any other input from the group."

The table was quiet, and Murray asked a question. "Thank you, Steve, Arne, and the whole team, for putting this list together. I agree with what you all have presented here. Have any of you had the opportunity to observe any of these teams in a training scenario or any capacity?"

Arne answered, "Yes, we have. You may know that one of our team engineers, Stan Kasperski, is a graduate of the U.S. Military Academy and used to fly the Army's Special Operations Black Hawk helicopters. Stan, you want to jump in on this?"

"Thanks, Arne. Yes, sir, Dr. Edgeton, after I graduated from West Point, I qualified for flight school and flew the MH-60 Black Hawk with the 160th Special Operations Aviation Regiment out of Ft. Campbell, the Night Stalkers. I've flown with Delta Force, Army Rangers, and the Navy SEALs on several missions. I have a lot of contacts with all of these groups, and we were allowed to visit several training facilities to observe some of these teams. We can all state, as we used to say in the Army, that these guys are the real deal. I'm a little biased towards our special operations teams; be they Army, Navy, Marine Corps, or Air Force; there are no better candidates, no one more highly qualified than what our military can offer. If you'd like, we can arrange a site visit for you at one of the training sites so that you can see first-hand what these professionals can do."

"Thanks, Stan, I might take you up on this. In the meantime, let me look at your proposal and supporting documents. At first glance, I think that you're all right on target. It's Tuesday, so why don't we look at finalizing this by Thursday morning so that we can get our selection process rolling? Appreciate all that you've done, very impressed."

As Murray and Nate were walking back to their offices, Nate asked, "I'm pretty happy with what the team came up with as far as our list of criteria goes, but I heard that they have already been formalizing a mission plan or something like that, based on what we had discussed in one of our earlier meetings. I will ask Arne to have their section get a mission plan drafted in anticipation of our approval of their criteria. Does that sound good?"

"Yeah, it sure does. Sorry, Nate, I'm just a bit preoccupied; my thoughts are a bit disjointed right now. I was thinking about something. I don't want you to think I'm out of my mind, but I'd like to participate in this mission."

Nate was a bit puzzled. "How do you mean? You're driving this mission. How much more could you participate?"

"I'm not making myself clear. I want to go." They continued walking down the hall.

"You can't go, Murray. First off, and no offense is meant, but you don't meet the criteria. You know the physical challenges of this, and as young and fit as you are, you don't meet the same standards as the SEALs. Plus, you really couldn't pass for a Mediterranean. Lastly, you are a once-in-a-generation genius. You could serve humanity more by doing what you're doing. I am not minimizing potential candidates' importance and individual worth, but we can't replace you. You can't go."

Murray looked at his friend, "I had to at least breach the subject. I thought it would be fascinating to see what all the fuss is about with this preacher from Nazareth." They walked back to their offices.

"Looks as if Murray and Nate like what we have done. I know that we were working on this earlier, so why don't we go ahead and finalize our, what did you call them, Stan, our 'Op Orders?'" asked Steve Oliphant.

"Yes, Steve, an Operations Order is developed in any military operation to give the unit the essential information they'll need to execute and complete their mission. My Marine buddies used to use what they call a '5 paragraph Op Order' that makes things pretty simple. It's known by the acronym SMEAC, which stands for Situation, Mission, Execution, Admin and Logistics, and Command and Signal. We can use this to help us focus our efforts, but what do we have so far? I know we developed our initial objectives for our project, but if we approach this from an engineering and a quasi-military perspective, we have much more work to do."

The Einstein Project team had completed a significant amount of work on developing the theory for time travel, but the actual planning for the execution of this project lacked the focus required for a project of this scope. Arne knew that as brilliant as Murray was, he was more concerned with testing his theories than looking at the real-world approach to executing a project. In light of this, Arne decided to task his engineering section with drafting a workable plan to bring this project online. His first decision was to talk with Nate and get him to champion Arne's efforts.

Arne arrived at Nate's office the following day after making an appointment to meet with him. Arne had known him for a few years and found him approachable and willing to listen.

"Thank you, Nate, for your time this morning," Arne started. "We have been working on this time travel project for the last two years, and the work we have been doing to develop these theories has been nothing short of amazing. But now that we're ready to kick the execution phase of this project off, I have to tell you that we are really short on developing workable plans for 'deploying a team' into the TLP. So much effort has been dedicated to research and experimentation that the crucial part of execution has become an afterthought. I'm an engineer, and we focus on doing stuff, but the timeline given for this project is approaching, and we're nowhere near complete."

Nate replied, "Arne, you have known me for what, three years now? You know that even for a theoretical physicist, I have a pragmatic streak." They both laughed at this. "What do you need, and what are your major concerns?"

"Nate, we're running out of time. I need you to ask Edgeton to leave our group alone so that we can work on developing a feasible and workable plan. We're talking about people's lives, for God's sake, and all of you up here in your Ivory Towers seem to have forgotten that present company excluded, of course. We need at least three months of working uninterrupted to create a workable plan. I know that you're a religious man, so excuse my language, Nate, but what the fuck! Has anyone asked us to do a 'what-if' analysis on this project? We spent two weeks, two fucking weeks, Nate, coming up with Krononauts. Krononauts for fuck's sake, two weeks! Someone has to get Edgeton to pull his head out of the electron cloud, along with pulling his head out of his anal aperture. It's interesting that we're considering putting a team into a time tunnel, but what if we put this team in the middle of an erupting volcano? I know that you theoreticians are all working on that, but let's say you all successfully transport a team into the same place we're standing right now, but it's 2,000 years into the past. That's great. Einstein was right, but once they get there, what do we do? That's where you have to let us have free rein to put a plan together for these guys once they get there. You know, little things like logistics, what supplies will they have? What if we put them into an active field of battle? What are the rules of engagement, the ROE? We have to look at a million things; we're hamstrung right now.

Arne paused to collect himself for a moment and then continued. "Here's another little question that has been gnawing at me: what are we doing this for? To go back and get a moon rock souvenir from the Middle East? Go to your local souk and grab something that'll save us a shitload of time and effort. I know I'm flippant, but what's our real goal here, Nate? Sure, we can return to the Middle East in the First Century, but why? Everything has already happened in the past; we can't change anything, and even if we did change something, what would that do to the future, you know, where *we* live? We're playing with fire, Nate. Do you remember when Oppenheimer looked at the firestorm in the New Mexico desert and quoted from the Bhagavad Gita, 'Now I become Death, the destroyer of worlds.' Doesn't this scare you?

"I'm sorry, Nate. I'm just venting a bit, but we need to ask you to champion our cause. We're all professionals and knew what we were signing up for, but we need to be given some time to put together a workable plan. Can you help us with this?"

"Of course, Arne, I'll champion your cause. I'll talk with Murray, and you and your team should be given what you need. You know, you talk about your being an engineer and how you engineers focus on doing things. Sometimes, we scientists forget about the proverbial nuts and bolts of things; what is that expression you all use where the rubber meets the road? To continue with that little cliché, we can talk about the vulcanization of rubber for hours on end, but isn't the young man in the tire shop putting a set of radials on my automobile more helpful to the public?"

Arne answered, "You know I would feel a bit better having that young man put tires on my car than some chemist down there trying to figure out how to turn a wrench. You know, I became an engineer because my dad was an engineer. My old man could solve more problems with his notebook and the slide rule he kept in his pocket than our group working with supercomputers. Well, that might be a bit of an overstatement of a loving son, but sometimes those engineers doing the grunt work in the trenches got more stuff done than all of us working in these nice, air-conditioned buildings. Damn, Nate, I sure am coming at you from all angles today, aren't I?"

Nate was very impressed with Arne's impassioned speech as he held some of the same views as Arne. He was content pursuing knowledge for knowledge's sake, and he felt that the work they were doing in exploring the space-time continuum was important. Still, he was concerned about exactly why his friend Murray was pursuing this project. Nate had an unsettling feeling that there was an undercurrent in Murray's drive, and he would breach this subject with Murray at the appropriate time. In the meantime, he wanted to get Arne's team what they needed to complete their work.

Three months later, Arne's engineering group delivered a highly detailed and workable plan for inserting a team into a Time Launch Point to be deployed to the Middle East in the First Century A.D.

Chapter Six

The first mission was developed. This was to be an insertion of a team of time travelers into the Eastern Mediterranean during the time of Christ. The mission was to test the thesis that time travel through accessing the TLP was possible. One of the most essential directives was that the insertion team was to observe only; they could do nothing to interfere with any events that occurred and then return to their time.

This presented an interesting opportunity for Murray. As an avowed atheist and anti-theist, this would allow him to demonstrate that Jesus of Nazareth was nothing more than a desert preacher from the backwaters of Judea. He, of course, would not publish this as his main objective, but this became for him a personal quest. Those old bible-thumpers, all that they could talk about was that Jesus is God, the second person in their Trinity. If Murray's theory was correct, if he could get back to Jerusalem in the early part of the First Century and demonstrate that Jesus was nothing more than a desert-dwelling itinerant preacher, then he could not be God. And if Jesus were not God, then the entire Christian argument would unravel—there is no God. He wanted to rub their smug faces into his proof. He'd show them, he'd get back at them, and he'd make them pay.

As he was thinking about this, Nate called and asked if he had time to chat about the project. Murray asked him to come over.

"Thanks, Murray. Something has been on my mind, and I wanted to discuss it with you. We both love knowledge for knowledge's sake, and the work we're doing here is more than just a love of knowledge. We are uncovering the mysteries of the universe and what makes the universe behave. Could you imagine what Einstein and Bohr could have done if they had the equipment that we have now? Well, we've got that equipment, and we're using it to the best of our ability to unlock some of these secrets. We owe it to later generations of scientists to further man's knowledge of the universe. We both believe that, and I believe that if Einstein had the equipment that we have, he would be there to do what we're doing in this project. This brings me to my question. Are we doing this for knowledge's sake? For science's sake? Why are we doing this?"

Murray sat back in his chair and looked very intently at his friend. "Of course, we're doing this to further science and increase our knowledge of how the Universe behaves. Why else would you think we would be doing this?"

"Well, you seem to focus quite a bit on Palestine in the First Century. I've even heard you say in one of our meetings with the team that maybe our 'Krononauts' could meet Jesus. That struck me as very strange as I know that you do not believe in Jesus or in anything that even hints at religion. Is there another reason why we're doing this? Do you have anything else in mind?"

"Nate, we're being presented with an unbelievable opportunity. We may have the ability to access the space-time continuum. We can prove Einstein was right about everything," he replied. "We can't change anything in the past, but maybe we can see into the future and find a solution to the brink of disaster that we find ourselves in all the time or even find a cure for the common cold."

"I know that we've already had these discussions with our ethicists. I know what you're saying, Murray, but be level with me; I'm the closest thing you have to a best friend. What is your real objective here?"

He answered, "Many people find our friendship a bit

strange. I respect your incisive mind, but you Indians all have a bit of a religious bent, and you know how I feel. You're always trying to wrangle some spiritual angle into our conversations; that's a bit strange, but do you know what I *really* find strange? How can you, as a physicist, actually believe in what Pink Floyd calls the Big Gig in the Sky? It's very baffling to me!"

"It was 'The Great Gig in the Sky' off of *The Dark Side of the Moon* LP, a fantastic album. Murray, we in India have found that science and spirituality can co-exist without problem. Pope Benedict even said a few years back that faith and science complement each other but are not mutually exclusive. And our history in India shows this. You may recall that the Kerala School of Astronomy and Mathematics flourished as early as the 1300s. Much of the work that was completed there was undertaken by Hindu monks. Murray, we were developing theorems and proofs for trigonometric functions in our attempts to solve astronomical problems as early as the 1400s. But my point is you can be a physicist and a believer at the same time. Look at Copernicus and Einstein. Both believers. Copernicus was a priest! Another Catholic priest, Father George Lemaitre, developed the Big Bang Theory. Look at the impact of Catholic priests on astronomy. I have a better question for you: how can you so quickly and completely dismiss the existence of a Supreme Being?"

"It's easy. Prove to me that there is a Supreme Being. Give me some proof. You know that as scientists, we have to be able to test our theories and have quantifiable, testable data to back up our claims. How does anyone know that a Supreme Being exists? How can anyone prove it?"

Nate smiled at his friend. "It's like the old saying, 'I have never seen the dark side of the moon, but I know that it's there.' But let's get back to my question: is there any other reason why we're embarking on this project?"

Murray almost jumped out of his chair, "You know there is, Nate. You know that I deny the existence of a Deity, and for the most part, I can't stand anyone who espouses a belief in anyone up there. Yeah, there's another reason that I want to go to Jerusalem in the First Century of *the Common Era*. I want our team to meet your Jesus of Nazareth face to face and then come back and tell the entire world that Jesus of Nazareth did exist, but he was nothing more than a minor footnote in history. He was nothing more than a desert-dwelling itinerant preacher and a rabble-rouser against the local authority. Remember that I told you I wanted to go on this mission? Here's why I could get real satisfaction from walking up to that preacher and laughing in his face because I would know that he was just a big fraud played on humanity, and I would expose it. That's it. That's my real motivation. If we can prove to the world who Jesus was, we'll be doing the world a favor. Think about it, Nate. How much hatred and war are caused by religious fervor, 'my God is better than your God' kind of bullshit. It's unbelievable. If we can eliminate religion, we might finally get some world peace."

Nate was looking at Murray in a different light. "OK, that's fine. But let me ask you a question: let's look at the reverse of your argument. What if the team goes back to Jerusalem and meets Jesus and finds that He truly is the Son of the Living God. What if they brought back some tangible proof? Would that change your mind?"

Dr. Edgeton thought about this for a while. "Sure, I'd be open to that possibility, but I'm not too worried about it; there won't be any proof because, as we used to say out in West Texas, there ain't nothin' there."

"Oh, my dear Murray, what's it going to take? OK, I have to get to a meeting. We'll catch up later on." With that, Nate walked out the door.

After Nate left, Murray thought that what his friend was telling him was not much different than what Jill told him when they had their falling out. Murray thought that what she told him was what led to their breakup. They spent the weekend in Santa Barbara at a beautiful bed and breakfast right on the ocean. After growing up in West Texas, he could not get enough of looking at the Pacific. That morning, they planned to take a walk down by Stearn's Wharf and then drive up to Solvang and the Santa Ynez Valley, but it didn't work out as they had planned. The

Einstein Project had been making significant strides in its work, and they were confident that a breakthrough would be very close. Murray was out on the patio having a morning Cappuccino when Jill joined him after her shower. "Can I get you a Cappuccino or a cup of tea?" he asked as she came outside.

"In a bit, let me just look at you for a moment. Wait a second, let me get my camera. The ocean is right over your shoulder. What a great shot, be right back." Jill came back and was snapping pictures of Murray with the ocean in the background. She found him so handsome, and she thought about how stimulating their talks were. She remembered debating with him during a meeting once; she knew she did better than him and made her points more convincingly. To this day, she would still jokingly needle him about it. She was sure that she was in love with him and that he was in love with her, but she sensed a slight undercurrent in his personality that she couldn't put a finger on. This was their first weekend together in a while, and she hoped they could have talked more about where they were going with this, but as usual, his mind was still back in Pasadena. "Penny for your thoughts, Sweetie?"

"Oh, what?" Murray was shaken out of his thoughts for a moment. "I was just thinking about the Project. We're almost on the verge of a breakthrough. I can feel it."

"Come on, Baby, not right now. We have to head back to Pasadena tomorrow morning, and I was hoping to keep the JPL as far away as possible. There is a nice little restaurant right off of Cabrillo that is supposed to have the best crepes in Santa Barbara. We could have brunch there after our walk, so I made reservations at 11:00."

"Sure. We can head out for our walk, and we'll head over to the restaurant. Sounds nice, but I was hoping to share with you what's happening with the Project while we're getting ready."

"That's fine, but only while we're getting ready. When we're taking our walk, I was hoping to talk about other things, OK? What breakthrough do you think you're all on the verge of making?"

Murray smiled at her, thinking that he got his way. "We think that we're almost on the verge of predicting when and where the Time-Launch Portal will open. I think that we will be able to do this. We can access the space-time continuum and send a team back into time. We can prove that Einstein's theory was right!"

"OK, so you can access the space-time continuum, then what? I've been thinking about this quite a bit. What would be the purpose of going back in time?"

He almost jumped out of his seat. "We could prove Einstein's work, we would add to the body of knowledge, we'd be doing this for the sake of science. We'd be unlocking secrets of the Universe. What more noble goal could there be?"

"But what if your time travelers get involved with what is occurring locally during their travels to the past? How are you all addressing the possibility that they can change future events?"

"We've been looking at that, and one of our primary directives is that they cannot do anything to interfere with events occurring on the ground. The entire team is in complete agreement with that."

"That's a big leap of faith, Murray. I'm not talking about actively interfering with events; I'm saying that just *sending* a team of observers into the past can have far-reaching consequences. The concept that you physicists call 'causality' is related to one of our principles in chaos theory; Lorenz called it 'The Butterfly Effect,' remember? An extremely slight change, what we would consider an insignificant change in the grand scheme of things, in the initial conditions, could create a significantly different outcome. Recall Lorenz's analogy: a butterfly fluttering its wings in a distant land could cause a tornado in Kansas. What you all are doing could have catastrophic changes in any future state. Doesn't this concern you?"

"Of *course,* it concerns me. That's why we're taking all of this into account. We're running models and simulations; we're doing all of that. Our time travelers will be under stringent orders to be as unobtrusive as possible and not to interfere with anything during their mission into the past."

"Murray, listen to me. I've been thinking about this project and what you're all doing. I must tell you this, you may be doing more than just opening Pandora's Box. What if you send your team back into time, and someone moves one rock out of place? What could happen? Someone could be walking down the path they have taken every day for the last ten years, the same path that has not changed. Then, one morning, they walk along this same path and trip on the rock that one of your team members inadvertently moved. That person trips and breaks his neck and dies. That person was supposed to be the father of a great general who maintained peace in the region in the years to come. Now, that general would not be born, and peace in the region would not be achieved, on and on and on. The Butterfly Effect, one slight change, and everything is changed. You have to consider what may happen. I'm telling you, you and your group should consider that maybe you should not pursue this until every contingency is considered."

Murray became visibly upset. He jumped out of his chair and stood right in front of Jill with his fists clenched. "Not pursue this? *Not pursue this?* What are you saying? That's like telling Von Braun not to build a rocket to go into space. We are on the precipice of unraveling secrets of the Cosmos, secrets of our existence. The entire march of science has been pointing to this time and to what we are doing. And you sit there, so smug in what you're saying, telling *me* not to pursue that which must be pursued!"

Jill was shocked. She witnessed a complete change in Murray, a change that she did not like; she felt as if Murray had just slapped her, and she was looking at him in a very different light. "Murray, are you listening to yourself? I said that you all should consider holding off on what you're doing until further analysis is undertaken. I'm not being smug. I'm asking you to consider what I'm saying."

Murray calmed a bit, then slowly got up and walked back into the room, "I'll be getting ready for our walk. We can leave in about half an hour or so, don't you think?"

Jill was expecting, at the very least, an apology for his

outburst, but it was as if he didn't hear a word that she had said. For a moment, she saw a very ugly streak in an otherwise very handsome face; for a fleeting moment, she was unsure where she stood in her relationship with Murray. Something was telling her that there had to be something else under that very brilliant veneer of his. Her first inclination was that he was under tremendous pressure from the team to complete the project. That had to be it. She got up to go change.

*****

They were walking along West Cabrillo Boulevard heading towards Stearn's Wharf. Looking to their right, the Pacific Ocean was sparkling in the sunlight, a sailboat was on a heading to the southwest, gulls were calling above, and the sky was a deep blue. The sun was above the Santa Ynez mountains off to the east, and a gentle breeze was coming in from the northwest; it was a spectacularly beautiful day on the Central Coast.

"It is so beautiful out here. No wonder they call Santa Barbara 'America's Riviera.' I'm so glad we got this time away, aren't you, Sweetie?" Jill asked as she was trying to smooth things over. Murray would normally take her hand in his as they would walk down the street, but this morning, he didn't; he was obviously still upset with her over what they discussed at the patio table.

"Yeah, it's nice. I'm glad that you're enjoying yourself."

She laughed and answered, "Of course, I'm enjoying myself. I'm glad to be out here; I'm exactly where I want to be; I'm with you. I thought we needed this time together without all of the interruptions from everyone back in Pasadena." Sensing that he wasn't listening, she said, "But I'm feeling that you'd rather be back there, am I right?"

Murray was subdued and didn't answer right away. He just kept looking at the path ahead of him. "I don't know, Jill. I have enjoyed being out here with you, don't get me wrong, but I have so much to do with the Project, and we are very close to making a major breakthrough; I guess I have been a bit preoccupied."

She thought that was about as close as she could get to an apology. "Sweetie, let me ask you something. We have been dating for over a year now. Where are we going? Is there any future for us?" Her eyes were instantly moist with unshed tears. She could not understand this huge surge of emotions; she had never experienced anything like this, and then she realized she was in love with him and wanted more than what they had.

"I thought that we had a nice thing going, Jill. We both enjoy our time together, and there are so many times that we will talk non-stop for hours on end; sometimes, I think we use up all of the oxygen in a room by talking so much. I still find our talks incredibly stimulating—"

"Is that all that you find stimulating, Sweetie?" Smiling as she tried to hold back her tears, Jill was trying to lighten the mood with him.

"Well, there's that too," he smiled at her and continued with what he was saying, "all that we do together, it has been nothing short of incredible. I think that there can be a future for us. I want a future for us, but I need to get this off of my chest. This morning, I felt as if you attacked me when you were talking about my work."

She put her hand on his shoulder to stop him, and she turned to him, "You feel as if *I* attacked *you*? How can you say that?" As quickly as her eyes became moist, they dried up, and like a lightning strike, her eyes flashed with anger. "Murray, what's going on with you? I raised a legitimate concern to you and asked you to *consider* what I was saying. I didn't demand anything from you or attack you. And how did you react? You said I was sitting there, all smug about what I was saying. Then, when I tried to respond, you walked out on me." She took a moment to collect her thoughts. "What do you expect from me, Murray? Do you have any idea how much you're confusing me?"

He rolled his eyes and replied with a hint of exasperation, "You're overreacting, Jill. You told me that I should not pursue my work."

"Overreacting? I never said that you should not pursue your work. But for the record, let me say that I saw a very different side of you, Murray, something I have never seen, and I have to tell you, how you reacted to me frightened me. I thought that for a second, you could have become violent with me."

"Now you're really overreacting. I would never become violent with you. I didn't like how you intimated that we on the Project Team have not thought things through. We have thought things through, and I don't need a non-physicist from an inferior school telling me that we haven't." As soon as the words were out of his mouth, he knew that he made a horrible mistake. He had no idea why he said that to her.

Jill was stunned. She had no idea who this person was in front of her. *'Inferior school?' Does he think that of me?* In a very calm voice, she said, "Murray, this morning, after we talked at the table, I thought that maybe we had a misunderstanding. I know how important your work is to you and you know that I have supported you wholeheartedly, both professionally and personally. Now that we're out here walking along the ocean, I thought we could enjoy ourselves, but as soon as I asked you if you were happy that we came out here, you began talking about the project. Everything is about the project. Why is this damned project so important to you? It's not about science; it's something else. When I asked you what was wrong, you blamed me. Then what do you resort to in the end? You insult me. I may be a 'non-physicist,' but I am sure you remember that the basis of physics is mathematics. You can do mathematics without physics, but you sure in the hell can't do physics without math. And you think that I went to 'an inferior school?' Is that what you think of me? While MIT is a very esoteric academic institution, and you all sit around in your little groups complimenting yourselves with your mental masturbation, and then you'll all talk about *doing* things, we graduates of inferior institutions like Georgia Tech will actually *do* them. Murray, I don't want you to think that I'm overreacting, but please take me back to Pasadena. I think that we're done here."

Murray shrugged his shoulders and replied, "Whatever you want." They didn't talk to each other during their two-hour drive back home. Later that week, he tried calling her several times, but she never answered.

Chapter Seven

As the Einstein Project finalized its selection criteria, they began searching for potential candidates. The pool of candidates was relatively large; there were more than 10,000 members in the military's special operations forces, but three candidates played a key role in this project. The events that unfolded turned on their actions just as the action of three gears turning together in a pully lift a massive load.

Summer Olympic Games
Beijing, China 2008

Midshipman Declan O'Sullivan, a physics major at the U.S. Naval Academy, was a gymnast on the Academy's gymnastics team whose first-place performance at the U.S. Gymnastics Championships secured him a spot on the 2008 U.S. Olympic Team. His overall performance as a gymnast was outstanding, but it was his performance on the rings that had him favored to win the gold. A very strong Chinese team combined with sustaining a slight injury before his event prevented him from winning a medal, but nevertheless, he still placed fifth overall.

He came from an Irish-Catholic family from South Boston and as a youngster, he was imbued with a strong sense of his Irish identity. He learned all about his family's history, starting with the O Suileabbhain clan, originally from the Celtic Province of Galicia, Spain, to the modern-day O'Sullivans who lived in all four Irish Provinces and throughout the New World.

His family also had a tradition of military service. His grandfather, Brian O'Sullivan, served as a U.S. Marine in Korea and was at the Chosin Reservoir in late November 1950. Returning home in 1952, Brian joined the Boston Police Department and retired thirty years later from the Bureau of Investigative Services, Criminal Investigation Division as a Detective Lieutenant.

Declan's father, Michael Sean O'Sullivan, served as an Embassy Marine in Spain, where he met Declan's mother, a young Catalonian woman named Ariadna Coixet Ocuna. He and Ariadna got married and moved back to Boston.

Being accepted to the U.S. Naval Academy, it was expected that Declan would continue the family tradition of serving with the Marines, but while at the Naval Academy, Declan developed an interest in the Navy Special Warfare Community, the Navy SEALs. During one of his midshipman summer cruises, he had the opportunity to attend the Naval Academy's "Mini BUD/S course." This course was extremely rigorous, but with his being a world-class gymnast, he was able to complete this program without too much difficulty. After completing this initial SEAL program, he was, as they say, "hooked" on this career path, and his goal was to become a Navy Special Warfare officer. Upon graduating from the Naval Academy and receiving his commission in the Navy, he attended the eight-week long "Naval Special Warfare Preparatory School," which was a mini-course designed to prepare aspiring SEAL candidates for the physical and mental rigors of attending the Basic Underwater Demolition/SEAL training program, commonly known as BUD/S, the demanding initial training course for the Navy Sea, Air and Land Teams, the Navy SEALs. While the prep course was much more difficult than the Mini BUD/S course that he attended while at Annapolis, he was able to complete this course towards the top of his class; he felt very confident about attending SEAL training. After completing the prep course, he competed for and received a spot at BUD/S in Coronado, CA.

He joined one hundred fifteen other SEAL candidates in Coronado to begin the first phase of this SEAL training. Almost a year later, only twenty-two candidates made it to graduation. Declan was assigned to Bravo Platoon, SEAL Team Three in Coronado, and continued with his training. He was serving with his platoon on a deployment to Iraq when he came to the attention of the Einstein Project.

Alqosh, Iraq

The family of Ashur Toma Boudagh, called "Tomy" by his family, fled northern Iraq in 1992 during a mass exodus of Christians from the Middle East. Alqosh, a village in the Tel Kaif district on the Nineveh Plain, is about 27 miles north of Mosul. Mosul is Iraq's second-largest city and is the historic and cultural center of many of the Assyrian people. Across the Tigris River from Mosul is the ancient city of Nineveh, where the prophet Jonah preached.

The majority of the inhabitants of Alqosh are ethnic Assyrians, and almost all of them are Chaldean Rite Catholics, one of the more ancient Catholic Rites; St. Thomas the Apostle preached the Gospel of Jesus in this region 2,000 years ago. Alqosh is located in the northern portion of Mesopotamia and is the resting place of the Jewish Prophet Nahum.

Following the First Gulf War in 1991, many Chaldeans fled from Iraq, but the large majority of the Chaldean community in Iraq was essentially displaced beginning with the fall of Saddam Hussein in 2003 and continued with the rise of the Islamic State of Iraq and the Levant, ISIL. The Chaldeans were one of the primary targets in Iraq following the breakdown of Iraq's infrastructure, and this persecution of Iraq's Christians reached a high point in 2014 when ISIL fighters attacked and captured many cities and villages in the Nineveh Plain, including Mosul.

Tomy's family escaped to Greece as many Chaldeans

did in the early 1990s. For the majority of Chaldeans fleeing Iraq at that time, there were very few options available to them. Most refugees settled in United Nations refugee camps, or if they had the means, they could attempt to cross illegally into Europe. These people had to make a perilous and treacherous journey, crossing the border through the mountains and into Turkey. They then had to make the long trek through the Asian region of Turkey to the European region into Greece. After many months of waiting for sponsors, the family was able to settle in San Diego County where there is a large Chaldean community, this one centered around the Chaldean Catholic Cathedral of St. Peter in the San Diego suburb of El Cajon.

Growing up in El Cajon is where "Tomy" first heard of the Navy SEALs. For as long as he could remember, he wanted to be one. Growing up in San Diego County, he had heard about the exploits of the SEAL teams, both the real-life stories of the Navy SEALs and the glorified versions of the teams on the big and small screens, and his life dream was to be a SEAL.

He read everything he could about the SEALs and attended every public relations and recruiting event in which the SEALs were involved. By the time he was in high school, Tomy had developed into an outstanding athlete, and he played water polo at his high school; he began to prepare for BUD/S at a very early age.

While a junior in high school, he attended several recruiting fairs for the Naval Academy, Navy ROTC, and other academic institutions. His grades in high school were very high, and he scored well on his SATs. With his excellent school record, he applied to and was accepted as a midshipman at the University of Notre Dame's Naval ROTC unit, where he majored in Classical Studies with special emphases in Latin and Ancient Greek. He also spoke Aramaic, the language spoken by present-day Chaldeans and Jesus of Nazareth. As did many Chaldeans, he learned Arabic as a boy, so he had significant training in languages.

Still pursuing his dream to be a Navy SEAL, during his time at Notre Dame he had the opportunity to participate in a

SEAL camp that was held in San Diego during the summer. Following his graduation and commissioning in the Navy, he applied for and was accepted for SEAL training. His career path through BUD/S and to the SEAL teams was very similar to Declan's, but unlike Declan, Tomy was assigned to Delta Platoon, SEAL Team Four in Little Creek, VA.

During his time as a SEAL, he participated in several clandestine operations and was with the SEAL teams when, like Declan, he caught the attention of the Einstein Project.

Riverdale, The Bronx
New York City

Jonathan Kaplan grew up in Riverdale, a middle-class neighborhood in the northwest section of The Bronx, and could not wait until he could get out. Growing up in a family of reformed Jews, he had a religious upbringing, but he became very disillusioned with Judaism as a teenager and hadn't been to a synagogue in years. He drifted for a while following his graduation from high school, but he joined the United States Marine Corps in his early twenties. Something about the Marine Corps clicked with him, and he found his calling in life.

While at Marine Corps Recruit Training in Parris Island, North Carolina, the rigorous recruit training course that turns young men and women into United States Marines, it was discovered that Jonathan had an uncanny ability as a marksman with the M-16 rifle and M9 9mm pistol. He qualified as an Expert Rifleman and Expert Pistol Shot. He graduated from Marine Corps Recruit Training and the School of Infantry East at Camp Lejeune, North Carolina. He was assigned as a Marine Infantryman to the First Battalion, Fifth Marine Regiment, known in the Marine Corps lexicon as 1/5, at Marine Corps Base Camp Pendleton, California.

Deploying with 1/5 to Fallujah, Iraq, in early Spring 2004, Jonathan distinguished himself as an incredible marksman. He provided expert covering fire for his fellow Marines as they were maneuvering against the Iraqi insurgents. Due to

Jonathan's actions, Marines were able to successfully recover a number of their wounded comrades as Jonathan kept the Iraqi fire in check. His superiors recognized this, and as his tour in Iraq was near completion, he was ordered to the Marine Corps Scout Sniper School in Camp Pendleton.

But another interesting thing happened to Jonathan while he was in Iraq. He met a fellow New Yorker, David Asher from Brooklyn Heights, another Marine Infantryman with 1/5. David was an Orthodox Jew who wore a *kippah* under his helmet. Jonathan and David were talking one afternoon when David started talking about the history of Fallujah. "Do you have any idea about the history of this place? I mean, our history, do you have any idea?"

"What are you talking about? We don't have much history here. I heard that the Brits were here before World War II, but I don't think that the U.S. had much involvement in this region until now, I guess," Jonathan replied.

"Not the U.S., you putz. I'm talking about *our* history, the history of the Jews. Use your *Yiddisher kop* once in a while. Listen, I don't know how much you learned in Hebrew School in Riverdale, but in Brooklyn Heights, if you didn't learn about our history and traditions, you weren't part of the *mishpocheh*. I'm talking about this place, Fallujah, this country, Iraq. We're right here on the Euphrates River, the Fertile Crescent, the Cradle of Civilization, Babylonia, and all that stuff. But you're probably thinking that this place has been full of nothing but Muslims, and that's it, right? Wrong. After the fall of Jerusalem, Babylonia became the focus of Judaism for over a thousand years, *a thousand years,* Jonathan. This place is steeped in our history. This city, Fallujah, was known in ancient times as 'Pumbedita' and was home to several Jewish Centers of Learning. Did you know that the Talmud was written here? It's correctly called the *Talmud Bavli,* the Babylonian Talmud. The primary source for Jewish Law is the Talmud, and it was written right here. Scholars centuries ago could have been sitting right here where we are, sitting around and discussing The Law. Now look at what has happened, here we are, surrounded by Muslim extremists who all want our heads, Death to Israel, Death to America, and all that crap, and here we sit, two Jewish boys from New York talking about the Talmud, is this world a crazy place or what? Incredible."

Jonathan thought about what his friend said. Although he had learned and experienced Jewish traditions as a kid growing up, he did not have an appreciation of his Jewish history. Once again, he felt that uneasy gnawing in his belly about abandoning his faith. "I guess," answered Jonathan. "But I have to tell you, I have found a home in the Marines. Something about their warrior mentality appeals to me."

"Speaking of which, I hear that you got orders to sniper school, good for you," said David. "You guys might think that the Scout Snipers are really badass, but just like we're talking about our history and how the Marine Corps warrior mentality appeals to you, don't forget that we Jews also have a very strong warrior tradition. Actually, we have an unbelievable warrior tradition. Think about Gideon. He took 300 'valiant warriors' and kicked the shit out of a large force of Midianites. He was one bad dude. Then King David had his *ha-Gibborim*, his 'Mighty Ones.' Remember the stories of his thirty elite soldiers? Do you remember the Chief of his Mighty Ones, Josheb-Bassebeth? He killed 800 men in a single battle. Now that's badass. Eleazar held his ground against the Philistines at the battle of Pas Dammim. Remember how his comrades fled the field of battle, and Eleazar held his ground? Shammah stood his ground against the Philistines in the Field of Lentils. We have an incredible warrior tradition as Jews. Even better than the Marine Corps! Everyone attacks us, and we keep beating the shit out of them; nobody fucks with Israel. Remember that when you're back at Pendleton."

Several years after spending another tour in Fallujah as a Marine sniper, he returned home as an instructor at the Marine Corps Scout Sniper School. It was here that he caught the attention of the Einstein Project.

Chapter Eight

Dr. Edgeton, on the advice of his team, had decided to move his training operations to Warner Springs, CA, a small community in the California desert. The U.S. Navy has a training site in Warner Springs where it trains Navy and Marine Corps aviators in survival skills, so this area has a proven track record of success in training in a desert environment and under difficult and harsh conditions. The topography of this desert area was very similar to that of ancient Judea, and its proximity to the ocean made this site even more similar to Jerusalem. A mock city resembling ancient Jerusalem was built to add even more realism to the training scenario. Out of over 1,000 individuals considered by the Einstein Project team for inclusion into this project as members of the "TLP Insertion Team," a group of about fifty individuals was selected to attend the training course in Warner Springs.

Jerusalem West

A replica of a typical rural village in the 1st century A.D. Palestine was constructed in Warner Springs. This included the family dwellings that were common at that time. Each home was built with a stone foundation, and bricks made of mud were used to construct the exterior walls. The interior walls were a smooth finish of plaster that people could decorate with frescoes or leave plain. Each home had its central courtyard with smaller rooms opening off of the courtyard itself. Additionally, most homes had access to the roof, which served as another room for the family. As lighting inside most of these homes was poor, the roof was where most of the daily activities took place, such as preparing food, sewing, and weaving. During the heat of the summer months, most families slept on the roof as it was much cooler than the inside of their homes. The central courtyard was the center of social life in the typical home. In the courtyard, the typical family would have their mikveh, a small pool of water, normally rainwater, that they would use for ritual cleansing. There was also a cooking area, a sitting area used for social gatherings, and a small, covered area where they kept their animals.

There was also a small replica of the *Antonia Fortress*, the citadel built by Herod the Great, named for his patron, Mark Antony. The primary purpose of the garrison of the Antonia Fortress was to protect the Second Temple. The Fortress was essentially a city within the city with its own fire department, bakery, and judicial system. Additionally, it housed approximately 9,000 soldiers and support personnel in a system of troop barracks and officers' quarters. According to Christian tradition, the Antonia Fortress was where the Roman Procurator of the region, Pontius Pilate, had his praetorium. It was in this praetorium that Jesus was tried for sedition.

During this training period, the skills required to operate in the environment of First Century Judea were honed. They were instructed in survival skills specifically for that time and were exposed to the various animals and plants from that region. However, a very interesting part of their training was learning about that society's daily cultural and social aspects.

The trainees ate the typical Mediterranean diet of the time; for example, the typical family ate fruits and vegetables of the region, beans and other legumes, fish, and, on special occasions, they ate meat such as goat and lamb. The students were also taught about the dietary rules imposed by Jewish religious beliefs and how this impacted the typical diet.

The trainees also underwent an intense language course in Aramaic and an immersion course in Classical Greek.

Aramaic was the language spoken by the Jews during the time of Jesus. Jesus spoke Aramaic during His public ministry, specifically, the Galilean dialect, which was distinct from the Judean Aramaic spoken by the people in Jerusalem. Aramaic was spoken throughout Palestine and Syria, but with the Arabic conquest of these regions in the seventh century A.D., Aramaic was eventually replaced by Arabic. The Galilean Aramaic spoken by Jesus was a Western Aramaic dialect, which in modern times is spoken in some regions of Syria. The Assyrian people, for example, the Chaldeans, speak an Eastern Aramaic dialect; however, certain scholars are working to ensure that the Western Aramaic dialects, including Galilean Aramaic, do not become extinct.

One of these scholars, a professor of languages from Ma'lula, Syria, one of the few remaining places in the world where Western Aramaic is still spoken as a common language. He was contracted by the Einstein Project to work with the trainees, and he was more than willing to do this as it would expand the number of Western Aramaic speakers. The professor was assisted by a Chaldean Catholic priest from San Diego who spoke both Eastern and Western Aramaic dialects. In addition to learning Aramaic, the trainees also learned about the culture and customs of all of the peoples of the Palestinian provinces of Idumea, Samaria, Perea, and Galilee. This training was to supplement the specific training they had of the people of Judea.

The plan was for the team to portray a group of Jewish pilgrims from Greece who were making a pilgrimage to Jerusalem for Passover. There was a relatively large and thriving Jewish community in the Macedonian city of Thessaloniki, so a group of Greek Jews arriving in Jerusalem would not be out of the ordinary. Thessaloniki was also home to many different groups of people from the Mediterranean area. The trainees selected to attend the training in Jerusalem West were of many different Mediterranean ethnic groups including those of Greek, Italian, and Arabic descent. A group of pilgrims from Thessaloniki could be comprised of many different

Mediterranean ethnicities, so this group of "pilgrims" would not appear to be anything unusual.

In addition to being trained in the village and city environment, the trainees were also taught to replicate a group of nomads traveling through the desert and to utilize materials specific to that time to erect their tents. As many diseases and other health issues were associated with that time and place, special instruction was given on first aid and disease prevention. While the military's special operators receive significant emergency medical training, each team has one medic/corpsman assigned as their primary medical asset. These specialists were given advanced training in diseases and health hazards endemic to the area.

The last area that was to be covered was their mission. Their mission was to travel through the Time Launch Portal to ancient Palestine, specifically, the province of Judea, demonstrating that time travel was possible. They also had a secondary objective of observing certain historical individuals from that era, specifically Jesus of Nazareth, and to determine what, if any, historical significance this Jewish preacher may have had. Was this man simply a charismatic teacher, or was there something more? Special emphasis was once again given to the other important caveat of their mission. This was their "primary directive," which was not to interfere with events that occurred while the team was performing their mission. Any interference could have a considerable impact on future events, so each member understood that there could be no interference of any kind. This caveat was the most significant part of their mission. Lastly, the ethicists with the Einstein Project discussed that in addition to the strict order not to interfere with events that would occur in ancient Palestine, the TLP team would not be able to carry modern firearms and ammunition with them. This led to a significant discussion with the project members. The possibility existed that the TLP team would encounter hostile forces and have to be able to defend themselves. As the TLP team would consist of only sixteen members, it would be impractical to send them in with no way to protect themselves, so a compromise was made that if the TLP team did encounter armed opposition, they would be able to defend themselves with non-lethal ammunition and non-lethal pyrotechnics, similar to what various municipal police departments use for crowd control.

Several members had argued that utilizing modern pyrotechnics was tantamount to interfering with events in the past. A biblical scholar who was an ad hoc member of the Project brought up an interesting counterargument: In ancient Palestine, the people who lived in the desert were very spiritual people who believed in supernatural phenomena. There were numerous instances throughout their history of prophets and what people thought were visitations from celestial beings such as angels. Using a non-lethal pyrotechnic to the people of that time would look like a supernatural phenomenon. It would not be considered something out of the realm of possibility, so the decision was made to allow the team to use non-lethal means to defend themselves.

With the majority of the planning completed and the protocols developed for the TLP team, the decision was made to proceed with the insertion into the TLP. The intense six-month training program was completed, and a team of the top sixteen graduates and sixteen alternates were selected to be members of the TLP team. This number was modeled after a military special operations platoon of sixteen members.

The selected members met all of the criteria established by the Project Team, and all appeared to be individuals from the Mediterranean.

The first group headed by Declan included Marine Sniper Jonathan Kaplan. The third member of this group was Navy SEAL Kevin Comeau, who was of French and Algerian descent. Kevin was born in Chicago, the city his family settled in when they arrived in America, where there is a sizeable Algerian ex-pat community. He spoke fluent French, Berber, and Arabic. His Arabic language skills served him well during his tours in Iraq while he gathered much-needed intelligence.

The other member of this team was a member of the

elite Air Force Special Operations combat rescue team, Pararescueman (PJ) Joshua Romano. Josh's family was descended from the Roman Jews, the *Yehudim Romim*. During World War II, his family took refuge in one of the many convents in Rome. Because of this, his family echoed the sentiments of the Great Rabbi of Rome, Elio Toaff, regarding how the Church hid and rescued thousands of Jews in Rome during World War Two. Originally from Long Island, Josh was one of the team's medical specialists.

The second group was headed by Tomy Boudagh and included Recon Marine Nick Stamnas, a first-generation Greek-American from New England who was fluent in Greek. The third member, Army Delta Force Operator Jerry DiCenzo, was of Sicilian descent. Jerry was also from the Midwest, coming from Cleveland, along with the fourth member of this group, Navy SEAL Kahlil "Kelly" Sabbagh from Philadelphia, whose parents were from Lebanon.

The third group was headed by SEAL Michael Parvanian from Los Angeles, who was of Armenian and Syrian descent; Delta Force Operator Brad Williams, a native-born Syrian, was orphaned during the war in Syria and was adopted by his American parents who lived in St. Louis; Delta Force Operator Miles Gomes from Miami whose family was from Brazil; and New Yorker Recon Marine Aaron Lieberman, a dual American and Israeli citizen.

The fourth group was headed by Army Delta Force Operator Ray Boutros, a New Jersey native who was of Coptic Egyptian descent; Recon Marine John Vasalo from Washington, D.C., who was of Maltese descent; Army Ranger Antoine Moannes, also of Lebanese descent; and Navy SEAL Sam Odeh. Sam, who was of Palestinian descent, was from San Diego and served as the team's second medical specialist.

Final preparations were made, and the calculations indicated that the Time-Launch Portal would be open within six months.

Chapter Nine

Insertion Point, Israeli coast, vicinity of Ashdod, 0245 Local Time

NASA had an arrangement with the Israeli government to use a secluded area along the Israeli coast as the "Insertion Point." It was at this point that the Insertion team assembled on the day that the TLP was calculated to be opened. They made their final checks of all of their equipment, which included mobile assets: battery electric powered dune buggies that had a range of approximately 300 miles, their standard Spec Ops weapons that had been modified so that they would be able to use non-lethal ammunition, other non-lethal weapons to include smoke grenades, "flash-bang" grenades and other support equipment. The sixteen team members were divided into four groups. This structure was based on the four-man fire teams employed by the Navy SEALs, and each group was assigned a vehicle. They were also dressed in local clothing based on archival records and local traditions. The vehicles were situated in a square, approximately two hundred yards from each other.

To add even more authenticity, a European donkey; there are fifty-one donkey breeds in Europe; and a wooden cart, a replica of carts used in the Mediterranean at the time of the First Century A.D., were to be transported with the team. The Einstein Project members named the donkey "Dapples," a tip of the hat to Miguel Cervantes' classic novel, *Don Quixote*. Don Quixote's companion, Sancho Panza, had a donkey named Dapples. The team could use the donkey and the cart to transport their load as pilgrims typically did during these times.

At first glance, the team members looked no different than a group of Middle Eastern or Mediterranean people from any point in time. Final calculations were made, and the team members and their equipment were placed in predetermined positions for insertion. The donkey was anesthetized and secured in the cart. A special hitch could be attached to one of the dune buggies to pull the cart, and then after they stowed their mobile assets in a predetermined location, the donkey would be harnessed to the cart.

There was a small transmitter tower that was roughly 2,000 yards from the "launching" position that transmitted real-time information to the control team. The local control team was in a monitoring station positioned approximately 10,000 meters from the insertion point and they were in constant contact with Central Control in Pasadena.

0430 Local Time

With local daybreak still a little over an hour away, all calculations were that the portal was going to open in 8.25 minutes. The team was assembled inside their vehicles as per protocol and their equipment was all stowed appropriately. They were in constant communication with the control team and their vital signs and other biological measurements were being monitored by Pasadena. At insertion, it was anticipated that all contact would be lost until recovery which was scheduled for nine days from insertion. The time clicked down for the next several minutes and then a low-frequency hum could be heard throughout the area. Looking eastward over the desert, a greenish, blue haze began to appear in what looked like a false dawn, and then what appeared to be a borealis type of wavering light appeared on the western horizon. Declan wondered if these were the "warning signs" that were supposed to occur prior to the opening of the TLP. A random thought occurred to Declan as he was awaiting the insertion, he thought about one of his midshipman summer cruises. He sailed in an Arleigh Burke class destroyer, USS *Mustin,* in the Western Pacific, and during this cruise, he witnessed the most amazing sunset that he had ever seen. He was surprised to see that what he was seeing was as incredibly beautiful as what he had seen that one summer at sea. The greenish, blue haze that he had seen initially in the east had changed rapidly to a deep purple, and then, incredibly, it changed to a deep red. Then the sky began to light up in a way that he could only describe as light twinkling on the waves over the Western Pacific Sea. Then the light both to the east and to the west began to shimmer like the Borealis light he had seen off to the west a few moments before. This "light show" continued for what seemed like an eternity and then…

0438 14 seconds Local Time

Suddenly, all of the team members could hear the hum intensify and see the bizarre behavior of the light. Right before the exact insertion time, they began to experience a significant shaking in their vehicles, and then almost immediately, what sounded like a huge rip in the earth occurred, along with a massive "whooshing" sound. Then they felt themselves accelerate at a tremendous speed into what looked like a tunnel with what appeared to be streaks of light at the top of the tunnel and the bottom. In what could be described as a sensory warp, they could see trailing images of themselves and each other. The acceleration continued and they felt pressed against their seats and were unable to move. This continued for what felt like an hour, and then, similar to a curtain falling rapidly to the floor of a stage at the end of a play, all of the lights went out. As rapidly as this had started, it ended.

Landing Point, 33 A.D.

It was still dark when Declan awoke. He took account of his surroundings, saw Jonathan next to him, and then realized where he was, or at least he thought he knew where he was. Gradually, he could make out two other vehicles and began to follow his protocol. His first job was to contact and rally the team. His solar-powered communication device emitted a soft LED light to let him know it was operational. His device could operate in radio-to-radio mode, and he could contact section leaders Tomy and Ray; they and their teams made it through the portal, but there was no sign of Michael, Brad, Miles, and Aaron. Protocol mandated that they wait up to an hour for the other elements to arrive, so they were in for a slight wait. Secondly, Declan had to perform a quick "low-tech" observation to determine if they had made it through the portal. Declan's background in physics let him know that they should still be geographically right outside of Ashdod; they weren't far from where they left; it was just that now they were separated by 2,000 years. He used his radio to see if he could contact the control team. He knew that the radios were working as he could contact Tomy and Ray, but there was no other signal on the radio. Then, Declan surveyed the area. The ocean was right there to the west, but the first thing that he noticed that was different was that the transmitting tower that was roughly a mile from their insertion point when they "launched" was no longer there. Either they made it through the portal and were in First Century Palestine, or they were transported to another geographical location in the present time. He would perform his second check in a moment to determine their position and that should confirm their transit. But first things first.

Declan checked on his teammates and began to inventory their gear. Two of their ammunition cases were lost in transit so they were down to what ammunition they had on hand plus the one small ammunition box that Declan had in his vehicle. Declan found that everything else was fully operational. Getting up out of his vehicle, he walked up to Jonathan, who was standing off to the side, "Well, what do you think? What did your trained eye pick up in that transit?"

Jonathan was still somewhat dazed by his experience and offered "It was hard to keep my eyes open, I must have passed out. That ride was insane, better than any ride at Coney Island. So, where are we? Do you think that we all made it?"

"We'll find out where we are, but my first thought is that we should be exactly where we left from, but let's try and figure this out. I counted two vehicles besides ours, and I was able to contact Tomy and Ray; they're all set. It looks as if Michael and his guys have not made it through yet. We still have a bit of time to see if they will make it, but all that I know is that they're not here right now."

Tomy walked up to Declan and Jonathan, a bit dazed but in good shape. "Looks like we made it. Did we go anywhere? What do you think, Deck? Did we prove that Einstein was right? Are we in the past?"

"I was telling Jonathan we should be exactly where we launched from," replied Declan. "My initial thought is that we did make it through, and we did travel through time."

Tomy asked, "Why do you say that Deck? We could have been moved fifty miles from the launch point, but we're still in the present."

"OK, check it out. If we are exactly at the launch point, which we'll find out in a minute, where is the transmitting tower? It was right over there," he pointed to the east, "but where is it now? The water is right there to the west, and we're still here in a desert area, so at first glance, it looks as if we haven't moved. Think about our transit. Did you feel the vehicles moving, or was everything else moving by us?"

"I don't know," answered Tomy. "It felt as if we were being pushed back into our seats by our acceleration. It felt as if we were moving."

The three of them, Declan, Tomy, and Jonathan, thought about what they had experienced, and they could not answer Declan's question. Tomy said, "You're the Team Leader, Deck, let us know what you want to do."

Declan assumed that they were still geographically outside of Ashdod. This gave him his "assumed" dead reckoning position that they would use to confirm their geographical position. He also surmised that Michael and his unit were also close by, but they may have been delayed or arrived early. Their protocol specified that they would leave a marker behind to let the other team members know that you were there and would meet them at the rally point, so maybe the rest of the team was still in transit. They'd find out sooner or later. In the meantime, while all of the team members were well-schooled in land and celestial navigation, one of the teammates, Kevin, was tasked with being the main navigator, and as such, Kevin was tasked with finding out where they were.

Kevin had a preprogrammed, solar-powered hand-held calculator to assist him with navigation. His calculator was a specially modified navigational device, similar to the TI-Star Pilot 89T, that had programmed the applicable Nautical Almanac and Sight Reduction Tables required for celestial navigation in its software. It also programmed the required chronograph set to Greenwich Meantime, which would also be necessary for determining their position. The calculator also had programmed dates listed back to the First Century. As this equipment operated without modern-day GPS satellites, Kevin used a sextant to manually verify the device's calculated position.

Kevin used Polaris, the North Star, to determine their latitude and quickly calculated that they were roughly 32 degrees north. Finding their longitude would be a bit trickier, but with the equipment that he had with him, he would get it. In the meantime, they knew the water was due west of them, so they began organizing themselves for their trek east.

He calculated their longitude, and it was approximately 35 degrees east. As Declan had surmised, they were still near Ashdod, right where they entered the portal. "Hey, Decker, you were spot on. I think that we're exactly where we started from." Their time was up waiting for the remaining teammates, so a marker was left for them to let them know where to meet the rest of the team.

The plan was to head towards Jerusalem and hide their vehicles in the Central Mountains. They aimed to travel as much as they could at night to avoid being observed. Although they knew that they only had about an hour before dawn, with any luck, they could get to the mountains before then. They headed east, keeping the prescribed distances between vehicles, and they made good time getting to the mountains. The cart holding Dapples was bouncing over the terrain. Tomy noticed Dapples was beginning to stir, but the beast was still asleep. The team located the predetermined location to store their mobile assets: small, uninhabited caves in the Central Mountains. Storing their dune buggies, they decided to rest a bit before heading toward the city. They looked back at the way they had just come and noticed that they did not leave any tracks as the wind was doing its job of rearranging the landscape. They planned to head east from the coast to Jerusalem, approaching the city from the northwest. The port city of Joppa was geographically north of their landing point of Ashdod. Joppa was where most shipping from Thessaloniki made landfall; a group of Greek pilgrims approaching Jerusalem from the northwest would not arouse any suspicion. The Einstein Project, working with the University of Pennsylvania's Museum of Archeology and Anthropology curator of ancient coins, fabricated exact replicas of Greek coinage from that time, obels, drachmas, and dekadrachmas, that the team could use during their mission.

They completed their preparations for their hike into Jerusalem. They took a complete equipment inventory and then waited for Dapples to recover from the anesthesia. After twenty minutes, Dapples awoke and was not in a good mood. After Tomy fed and watered the animal, they put the harness on Dapples and hitched him to the cart. All their equipment and supplies were loaded onto the cart, and they made their way out of the Central Mountains.

As they walked, Tomy sidled up next to Declan and began talking. "Deck, how do you feel about what's happening right now?"

"I guess that everything's going OK. I'm concerned about Michael and his team, but there must be a logical explanation for why they're not here right now. In the meantime, we'll carry on with our mission. Why, what's up?"

"Deck, I've been in the Navy long enough to know that we signed up for this and that no one put a gun to my head to be where I am right now, but there's just something about what we're doing that's giving me some doubts. I mean, traveling through time? This can't be right, Declan. When Columbus sailed into the unknown, they had a basic idea of what they were doing. All of that 'the world is flat' stuff was all bullshit. Sailors knew back then that they weren't going to fall off the edge of the world. Every time a ship sailed, people on the shore watched the ships sail over the horizon, and the ships returned to port. They knew that the Earth wasn't flat. The big unknown was what was on the other side of the horizon, but they had a basic idea of what was going on. Same thing with space travel, but what we're doing here, this is stuff that's completely unknown, and I've got an uneasy feeling that we're putting our dick-skinners where they don't belong, do you know what I'm saying?"

"Listen, Tomy, my degree is in physics, not philosophy. Well, maybe that's not quite right. Physics started out as a philosophy discipline, but we're like Columbus and those guys; we do have an idea of where we're going. Einstein theorized that this was possible. He showed how the space-time continuum could roll back on itself and portals could open that could allow traveling back into time. We've demonstrated that his theory was right; we *can* access the space-time continuum. Should we be doing this? I don't know. It takes courage to head into the unknown, but think about this: if the first guy didn't eat a cocoa pod, we wouldn't have M&M's today."

Tomy laughed at that with Declan, then turned serious and said, "Sure, that's true, but here is my main concern. Look, Deck, doesn't this concern you or make you at least think about what Edgeton and the rest of those guys in the puzzle palace are up to? Why is one of our objectives to 'gather info on Jesus and see what historical significance he has'? Why focus on Jesus? We're both Christians, and we believe in who Jesus is. Why is Edgeton fixated on this? Something about this stinks."

"Well, let me ask you this: what if the TLP were to open during the Exodus of the Jews from Egypt? Maybe Edgeton would have us see if the Red Sea really did part. I think that he's just dealing with the cards that he has. Since this TLP opened to

Palestine in the first century, he wants us to look at the most significant person to come out of that period."

"*Most significant person*? Listen to yourself, Deck, we're talking about Jesus, the only begotten Son of God! We might be going down a path that we shouldn't. I trust you, and I trust our team, but after seeing where we are right now and knowing what kind of person Edgeton is, I'm concerned. I don't trust any of those assholes back there."

"How about Dr. Joseph? He seems pretty much on the level. What do you think of him?"

Tomy said, "You're right; he is on the level. Forget it, Declan; I'm just a bit spooked right now. Something doesn't feel right."

"Let's just see what this day brings. We have a good idea of when the portal will reopen. Let's focus on our mission and figure out what kind of artifact we can bring back. Maybe Dapples will get lucky and find a female donkey that we can take back with us. There have to be some Middle Eastern donkeys around here."

"Honestly, Deck, you know that feeling we get when you know something is off, but you just can't put your finger on it? That's what I'm feeling right now, just something weird."

"That's good, Tomy, things are unpredictable right now. Remember what we learned back in BUD/S when the instructors taught us about 'predictability?' Predictability leads to expectation and complacency. Expectation and complacency lead to a loss of attention to detail. Loss of attention to detail gets us killed. If you feel that something isn't right, your senses are heightened, and that's what we need right now. Does that make sense?"

"Yeah, you're probably right. It might be what that one scholar back in Pasadena was saying: the people here were very spiritual, and there might be a good reason for that: the world's major religions came from this area. There is something about this desert that is beyond our understanding."

"Tomy, how many religion classes did you take at Notre Dame? Man, you're getting all ascetic on me. Are you waiting for Saint John the Baptist and the Essenes to jump out of the hills?"

"He just might. But along with the locusts and wild honey, I wonder if he'd have a cold beer with him. I sure could use one right about now." And with that, they walked on. They made their way towards Jerusalem but detoured towards the ancient city of Bethany and that was where they first encountered people.

Insertion Point, Present Day, 0530 Local Time
On the Israeli coast, vicinity of Ashdod, Israel

The local controllers were in direct communication with Central Control in Pasadena and had been trying to monitor the transit of all four sections. Their instruments reported a significant event that opened the portal at 0438 local time, and they were able to monitor the entry of the insertion teams into the portal. They could monitor all four sections, but something was wrong. They could monitor the four teams via disturbances in the magnetic field associated with their predetermined positions. While three teams stayed constant, one of their readings disappeared from their instruments. Readings indicated that three elements of the team were still associated with their initial positions, but there was no sign of the other group. The local controllers and Central Control both continued to monitor, and they were hoping that something would break for them soon. At present, the local controllers could no longer monitor any of the insertion teams, but that was to be expected. All that they could do at this point was wait until recovery. Back in Pasadena, Dr. Edgeton reviewed the feed from the recording monitors and analyzed the atmospheric phenomena that had occurred. The Borealis-like waves they saw to the west and the greenish-blue haze that had happened on the eastern horizon were similar to earlier accounts of TLP activity. They reviewed all data to determine their origin. Hopefully, this would give them even more insights into the space-time continuum.

Chapter Ten

Bethany, 33 A.D.

The entire town was alive with the news of what occurred:
The preacher Jesus had raised Lazarus from the dead before
dawn. He had been summoned by Lazarus' sisters to come help,
but Lazarus had died several days earlier. Jesus had ordered that
the stone that sealed Lazarus' tomb be removed. As soon as it
was moved, He entered the tomb. All those present could smell
the death and decay from the tomb as Lazarus had already
turned. But those at the tomb felt an unnatural stillness in the
air. Many had seen what they called "dancing lights" in the sky
as Jesus summoned Lazarus. The news spread like wildfire, and
people from all over the area descended on Bethany. Several
small groups of men had entered Bethany unnoticed in all of this
excitement.

Declan and Tomy were listening to the excited crowd
heading to a small hill on the outskirts of the town. Although
the entire group had undergone an immersion course in Aramaic
back in Jerusalem West, they could not follow what the villagers
were saying. The people were so excited and spoke rapidly and
with a local accent. All of the team members, except Tomy,
could only understand about half of what was said. Tomy,
whose first language was Aramaic, could understand everything
being said, and he told the rest of the team what he had heard:
Jesus raised Lazarus from the dead, and the Teacher and His
Apostles were still here with the villagers. The excitement in the
air was palpable, and they followed the crowd to the hill. The

team moved about twenty yards away from the villagers, just out of earshot.

"I can't believe this," Tomy told Declan. "This is something out of the movies. There is no disbelief in these people. They're undoubtedly excited, but it's almost as if they expected this to happen. Jesus is one of them, and they believe Him. I can't believe that we are here. This is incredible. Did you hear them talking about the dancing lights in the sky? Guess what that was? It had to be the cosmic phenomenon associated with the portal. This could be what I was talking about. Something was going to happen. I can't believe that we 'happened' upon this. It's as if fate is pulling us here."

"Slow down, Tomy, let's stick to what we're supposed to do. Let's focus, people." With that word of caution from Declan, they all tried to suppress their excitement. Jonathan knew his scriptures well enough to know that preachers and miracle workers were always present with the Israelites. Although he was a bit jaded and cynical, he could feel the electricity in the air and was taken up with it. He wished that his buddy, David Asher, was here with him. He'd fit right in. He walked over to talk with Declan and Tomy.

"Hey, guys, what's going on? What's this about Jesus raising someone from the dead? Help me out."

"Jesus performed many miracles during His ministry in Judea, but this one got everyone's attention," Tomy answered. "Jesus was friends with Lazarus and his sisters Martha and Mary. If I remember my Scriptures correctly, Jesus was teaching beyond the Jordan when he heard that His friend Lazarus was ill. The sisters Martha and Mary sent word to Jesus, asking Him to come. Jonathan, you know as a Jew that family and friends must come to pray with their relatives when they're sick. Martha and Mary had seen Jesus perform miracles, so they knew that if Jesus came, not only would He pray with them, but He could also heal His friend. But Jesus waited. He stayed beyond the Jordan for two more days; he waited for His friend to die so that He could come here to Bethany and raise Lazarus for the Glory of God the Father. By the time Jesus and His Apostles arrived here, Lazarus had been dead for four days and was already in the tomb. When Jesus arrived, the villagers were mourning with the sisters, as one of the sisters, Mary, was in the house sitting on the floor. I guess that she was still in shock from losing her brother and the fact that Jesus did not come to heal him."

"She was sitting *Shiva,*" said Jonathan.

"What's *Shiva?*" asked Declan.

"Oy, you goyishers. You know from nothin'. Shiva, it's a seven-day mourning period for the family of someone who has died. Shiva comes from the Hebrew word for 'seven.' It is the essential duty of the community to comfort the mourners. On the first day of Shiva, the community provides the meal after the burial. Mary was sitting Shiva; this is very important to us. When you enter the home of the family you recite '*Ha-Makom ye-nachem etchem be-toch she'ar avelay Tziyon vi-Yerushala'yim,*' this means 'May G-d comfort you together with all of the mourners of Zion and Jerusalem.' Men don't shave, women don't wear make-up, it's a very formalized process. For the family, it is very comforting."

Tomy jumped in, "Look around you, Jonathan. What do you see going on here? The rituals and the traditions that you learned as a kid, they're right here!" For Jonathan, something beneath the surface of his consciousness was trying to break out. Everything here was like a dream state for him; it felt like he had just woken up and was trying to remember a dream. There was something from his past that was catching up with him, and then it hit Jonathan like a slap across the face: he was a Jew, and he was in his ancestral homeland. Emotions began to well up in him, and it took all of his willpower to control them.

The crowd of villagers began to move. The team was dressed in clothes from that era, and like everyone else, they carried shoulder bags. However, unlike everyone else, instead of food and other supplies in their bags, they had weapons and other equipment. In their cart drawn by their donkey, Dapples, they carried more equipment, including their tent for sleeping out in the desert, food and water, and other supplies. They moved with the crowd towards the hill, and upon reaching the hill, they could see Jesus of Nazareth and His disciples walking away from the home of Lazarus and his sisters. Tomy was still a devout Chaldean rite Catholic and was visibly shaken by what he saw. Not only the fact that they had traveled through time, but to Tomy, these were his people, and that was Jesus in front of him. All of his training as a SEAL forced him to be neutral and objective, but 2,000 years of Christianity was in his genetic makeup. It was hard for him to control himself. He was experiencing the same feelings that Jonathan had, and he was also having difficulty containing his emotions.

Declan was reared as a Latin rite Catholic, although he stopped attending Mass on a weekly basis when he was at Annapolis. All these emotions bubbled up to the surface at that moment, and he was overtaken by emotion. As Team Leader, Declan had to quickly regain his composure. He immediately shifted gears as easily as he shifted gears on his classic Mustang and went into full SEAL mode. He had to display critical thinking and mission-oriented leadership. Quietly, Declan ordered the group, "OK, guys, spread out and observe everything, keep to yourselves, and keep conversations to a minimum." The entire TLP team had conversational skills in Aramaic and Greek, but as Tomy and one of the other team members, Ray, were fluent in both languages, they were to be the group's spokesmen.

The one thing that they all observed was that Jesus and His disciples were trying their best to get away from the growing crowd of people. Everyone tried to touch Jesus, and He talked to the people there. You could see that Jesus and His group were trying to make their way to Bethany itself, heading to the road leading south. Everyone noticed Lazarus and his sisters still by the tomb and ran to see them. You could see from a distance that Lazarus was disheveled and dazed, but he was obviously overjoyed to see everyone. He kept looking toward Jesus and where He and the disciples were heading. Lazarus could not move fast enough to keep up with Jesus, but their eyes met, and that was all it took. Jesus looked at Lazarus, and Lazarus knew what Jesus had done and why; Lazarus smiled, and his love for Jesus closed the distance between them. Then, the crowd was upon him. "Lazarus, Lazarus, tell us what happened!! What happened?" Lazarus sat down with his sisters, and Declan and some team members moved closer to hear what had happened. Lazarus began to explain, "About two weeks ago, I don't know what happened, but I became violently ill after eating and began to vomit everywhere. Martha and Mary tried to feed me, but nothing would stay down. I began to ache everywhere and became very feverish. After that, I don't know, the next thing I remember, the Teacher was standing over me, and I looked up at him and smiled."

Mary and Martha began to talk at once, with Martha taking over, "Lazarus began to shake, and he was burning up with fever. He could not eat or drink, and he was covered with sweat. We sent word for the Teacher to come as He could heal Lazarus. You all know how much the Teacher loved us, so we were sure He would come. Then Lazarus became so hot that he began to sweat blood. He turned white, and then he stopped breathing. He lay there a full day and night until the neighbors came to prepare him and have one of our male relatives recite the Mourner's Kaddish. Still, for three more days, the Teacher did not come. And then this morning before daybreak, as many of you were here with us, the Teacher arrived with His followers. I said to the teacher, 'Teacher, if You were here, Lazarus would not have died. But even now, I know that whatever You ask of God, God will give you.' And then He said something very strange; He said, '**Your brother will rise**.' And I told Him I know that Lazarus will rise on the resurrection on the last day.' But then the Teacher said, '**I am the resurrection and the life; whoever believes in me, even though he dies, will live, and everyone who lives and believes in Me will never die. Do you believe this, Martha?**' At that moment, I knew. I knew who He was. He is the Lord, the Messiah, who has come into the world to save us. I told the Teacher, 'You are the Lord!!' I then went to get Mary, who was still sitting shiva on the floor with the people who came to comfort us; I told Mary, 'The Teacher is here, and He is asking for you.' Mary then ran to where the Teacher was, and she fell at His feet, saying what I had said, that if the Teacher were here, Lazarus would not have died. The Teacher looked at both of us and asked where we had laid Lazarus. Mary showed Him where the tomb was, and He ordered those there to roll away the stone. I almost screamed, 'Teacher, please don't; he has been dead for four days now; he will already be rotting, and there will be a stench.' But He looked at me and told me, '**Did I not say that if you believe, you will see the glory of God? Please move, Martha, let Me go in. Your brother will be here shortly.**'

"They opened the tomb, and all of us could smell the rotting stench of death emanating from the tomb. Even though it was early morning and cool, the stench was overwhelming. Lazarus had been so sick that it seemed like he was already rotting. But the Teacher went into the tomb, and he began to pray, and then I heard the Teacher yell to Lazarus, '**Lazarus, come out!**' I didn't see them, but some people here said they saw dancing lights in the sky. The next thing I knew, there was Lazarus. He was still wrapped in his burial clothes. And if you go into the tomb, what can you smell? All that you can smell are the flowers! There is no stench! Look at Lazarus. What do you see? Do you see the same dead man we placed in the tomb four days ago? You all must know, who is the Teacher? He is the Lord!!" With that, they all looked toward the southern road. They could see Jesus and His disciples heading toward Bethany.

Tomy was unable to take this in. He could hear the anguish in Martha's voice when she was describing her sending word to Jesus and the conviction in her voice when she declared who Jesus was. Everyone there was stunned, but Lazarus kept looking toward Jesus with a look of pure contentment on his face. He looked as if he knew something, a profound secret, that no one else knew, but he would tell everyone what he knew about Jesus. Tomy walked up to Lazarus and began to talk to him. "My friend, I am not from these parts, but I have heard what happened here. What can you tell me about this Teacher?"

Lazarus looked at Tomy and said, "Your accent is different, I can tell. Are you Greek? Well, that doesn't matter. Yes, the Teacher, we have known Him for a long time and love

Him. He has always stayed with us when He was here in Bethany, and He has taught us many things about the love that God has for all of us and how we should love each other. It has been difficult to understand all that has happened today, but if you knew Him as we know Him, it may be difficult to understand, but it is easy to believe. When Martha said she knew who the Teacher was, she spoke for us all. I believe He is the Lord, the One promised to us by the prophets. He is the One who has come to deliver us, but He doesn't preach about delivering us from the bondage of the Romans. He preaches about delivering us from death. And death is a greater taskmaster than the Romans. Why don't you stay with us? We can talk more of this; you are more than welcome to stay."

"Thank you, sir. It is very kind of you to offer that to me. You are right, we are Greeks, and we are making a pilgrimage to Jerusalem for Passover. If I could stay with you and learn about the Teacher, I would. After Passover, might we come by again and hear of your Teacher?"

"Of course, we would welcome you and your friends. You were a witness to what happened here today. I can hear it in your voice; I believe that you may already know who our Teacher is, and in your heart, you know. You don't need to answer me. I can see it in how you looked at the Teacher. You know. I wish you a safe journey and I give you my *Shlama*."

Tomy heard this, and although he knew exactly who Jesus was, hearing it from these people was something that was alive. He had to stop and remind himself who he was and what he was doing there. It would be easy for him to leave the team and stay with Lazarus. He could follow Jesus and be one of His followers. Tomy was shaken out of his thoughts. He felt more than heard Declan next to him. Declan said, "I'm like you, Tomy. I was a believer before and even more of a believer now, but we have work to do. Let's get down to Jerusalem to observe what happens there. I need you to be able to speak for us. Let's get ready to pull chocks." With that, they headed on the southern road, following Jesus.

"Declan," Tomy began, "you have to admit, this is

mind-blowing. Can you believe what just happened? Were you affected at all by what we experienced?"

"Yeah, I do," Declan said. "I remember once, when I was a kid, my family vacationed in Rome. I was about fourteen at the time. Now, remember, I grew up pretty devout, having a strict Irish Catholic father and a mother from Barcelona. I had it from both fronts. The Spaniards call Spain "La Tierra de Maria," the land of Mary, and well, Ireland, of course, is the Holy Land. Back then, I loved the ceremony and the pageantry of the Church. I watched Midnight Mass on TV from St. Peter's, and once I saw the ceremony of the canonization of a saint, I found it majestic. But back to this trip, we landed at FCO, Fiumicino International, and caught a bus into Rome. My dad had connections, and we stayed at this incredible hotel right down the street from Vatican City. As we crossed over the Tiber River and turned the corner onto Via Concilliazione, there was St. Peter's Basilica right before me. I was completely speechless. Looking at St. Peter's was like looking at the entire history of your faith, your family, and your culture all in one glance; it was amazing. I felt the same way today, but a thousandfold. So yeah, this is mind-blowing."

"I'm thinking about our marching orders," Tomy reflected. "The team in Pasadena told us that this entire project will be classified for several years, correct? But do you remember when my sisters, Maria Teresa and Raffaella, visited me in San Diego when we had that four-day weekend off from Warner Springs? Many of us all headed down and spent a weekend in Encinitas. Do you remember them?"

"Yeah, who couldn't? Your sisters are both babes."

"No shit, Deck, Chaldean women, for the most part, are very beautiful, but back to what I was saying. This one engineer with the Project Team, I think that he is involved with optics and lasers, something like that, well he was crazy over my sister Raffaella, and he was trying to worm his way into my good graces, big brother and all, not to mention being a badass Navy SEAL. This guy invited me out for drinks one evening, hoping my sisters would be there, but no such luck. He gets his dumb ass pretty well hammered, and he starts talking about the project. I said to him, 'Hold off, shit for brains, you can't be talking about this in public,' so we headed outside on the patio and there was no one out there. We're outside, and he's trying to be all cloak and dagger-like. He told me that if we returned from this time travel and reported that Jesus of Nazareth was simply a preacher from the hinterlands, the project would likely be unclassified within a year. If we returned and had hard proof that Jesus is who we know He is, the project would never be declassified. That's what I was trying to tell you about earlier. This Edgeton guy is a fucking whack-job. Something about him isn't right. If you're trying to tell me that we can come all the way back in time to the time of Our Lord, and we can prove beyond the shadow of a doubt who Jesus is, why not proclaim it to the entire planet? Missionaries and evangelists have been proclaiming the Gospel for years with no proof except for their faith, and many of us are believers. We don't need proof, but how about people who are hungering for an answer as to what in the fuck are we doing on this planet? Don't you think that if we can answer that, the world would be a better place? Now I don't know if that engineer is full of shit and the beer was talking for him, but even before I talked with that guy, I had this feeling about our illustrious Dr. Edgeton."

"Tomy, you and I are just a couple of grunts on the ground carrying out our mission. You know the drill. But I agree with you. Why don't we try to find something, the artifact we're supposed to come up with? Let's try to bring something back that will bolster our case. But listen, although I was blown away by what we just saw in Bethany. I'm going to throw a bit of a wet blanket on your enthusiasm. As per our mission, let's continue doing our surveillance. You and I have a job to do; we are to gather information on Jesus of Nazareth, and that's what we're going to do. Let's gather as much info as we can. Let's write up an after-action report of what we witnessed in Bethany, and we'll get all the guys to corroborate it. That's doing our mission. We'll do this for every major event that we witness, and we'll have the guys record any other interaction that they have with the locals. We'll compile everything that we have, and we'll go from there. Does that sound fair?"

"Yeah, it does," Tomy said. "Don't worry, Deck, I'm all in on our mission, but you must admit, this is nothing like we have ever seen. Let me go back and check on the guys."

Declan was alone with his thoughts, and he was a bit conflicted. Yes, he did have a strong Catholic upbringing, and he was blown away by what he had seen in Bethany, but a little pessimistic seed of doubt was still bubbling up in his brain. What if what he had seen in Bethany had been nothing more than a coincidence? What if all that he had ever learned about Christianity was just the reporting of some overzealous evangelists? He didn't know what to think. His faith was not as strong and absolute as Tomy's; he had some soul-searching to do and was glad for the time alone.

As he was alone with his thoughts, Declan recalled something he had seen before they left Bethany. Declan, Tomy, and the rest of the team had recalled that Jesus and His Apostles were leaving the home of Lazarus and his sisters. There was a large gathering of people outside trying to get a glimpse of Jesus and Lazarus; because of the story of Lazarus, many of the townspeople were beginning to demonstrate a significant interest in Jesus and the miracles He was working. Declan noticed that as Jesus was walking towards the road heading south, He looked back at Lazarus several times, and when he was about one hundred yards away, He turned and waved, a simple gesture of friendship that conveyed a message of hope and love.

Declan could not know this, but at the time that he, Tomy, and the team were on the road to Jerusalem, some of the townsfolk had brought the news of Jesus raising Lazarus from the dead to the attention of the chief priests. One of the chief priests, Caiaphas, who was serving as the High Priest for this year, was hearing reports that Jesus was being proclaimed as a king. There was an uneasy peace between the Romans and the Jews, and the news of this Kingship of Jesus would undoubtedly cause problems for the Romans; they were very wary of anyone challenging the authority of Rome. Caiaphas began planning to eliminate this potential problem before it took root.

*****

Bethany was only about two miles from Jerusalem, and the team was able to arrive in Jerusalem in less than an hour; they had taken their time so as not to arrive in Jerusalem before Jesus and His Apostles. Upon arriving in Jerusalem, one of the first things they did was go to a money changer to exchange their Greek currency for some shekels.

"Hey, Tomy," Declan called Tomy over. "Look at these coins; they're freshly minted and in perfect condition. These can be some of the artifacts that we can bring back!"

"They could be. They look a lot better than anything in a museum. Hey, Deck, remember when I asked you if you ever had one of those feelings that something really bad was going to happen? Don't want to spook you, but I'm getting one of those feelings right now. Something very strange is going to happen. I can feel it."

Chapter Eleven

Jerusalem, 33 A.D.

The centurion opened his eyes in the darkness of his room. It was before sunrise, and although spring had arrived, his room was still cold. He turned onto his side, pulled the blankets back over his shoulders, and tried to burrow deeper into his bed. "Please, Somnus, let me have another hour more." Closing his eyes, he heard his servant, Larus, moving about in the courtyard, preparing the morning fire. The servant must have dropped something as a loud clang could be heard throughout his quarters. "I guess that Somnus didn't hear me." He threw his legs over the side and placed his feet on the cold floor. Sitting up in his bed, he saw Larus walking out of the darkness into the room with a basin of water and a towel.

"Oh, good, you're awake. Here, wash your face and clear the cobwebs from your mind. I started the fire outside, let it boil over, and then I'll bring a brazier to warm you up." He set the basin and towel on the nightstand. "Get up, Gaius Antonius. You have much to do today."

He looked at his servant and shook his massive head to wake up. Soaking the towel in the basin, he put it up to face and said, "I'm getting too old for this; my knees are killing me. This has never happened to me before; I need to retire and go back home."

"No, you don't. You need to get up and get yourself ready for your meeting this morning. I'll have your breakfast ready for you. I also have that salve that I prepared last week. I can put that on your knees to get your juices flowing." He walked back out to the courtyard and prepared a brazier to bring into the centurion's room. He brought the brazier over and set it next to the bed. "Here, this should make you feel better. I'll get that salve to put on your knees after you're dressed for the day. And one other thing, my fine Roman, you are not as old as me; you're just drinking too much lately. That's why your knees are hurting you this morning."

He got out of bed and threw his cloak over his back to ward off the morning cold. "As old as you are, you still haven't learned manners. I don't know why I keep you with me. I'd be better off with a new servant."

Larus was preparing the centurion's breakfast, and he laughed at his grumbling. "HA! Ask your children. You would be lost without me taking care of you. Speaking of which, when was the last time you heard from your family? Is your son still planning on joining you this year?"

"No. I asked him to start preparing our affairs for our move to Gallaecia. This will be my last year with the Legion. I will return to Rome next year, and then we will settle back in Gallaecia. I will spend the rest of my days in peace. Now, what do we have planned for this morning?"

"You see how you have to ask me what you need to do today? What would you do without me? You have to prepare your century for your assigned patrol duty at the city gates. Do you not recall that Yeshua will be arriving in two days for Passover? That's all that everyone is talking about on the streets. You have been assigned to maintain order at the gate. I'll ready your uniform, eat your breakfast. Do you need me to bring you some wine, or can you make it through the morning without it?"

The centurion sat at the table and grunted. "Yes, bring me some wine. That's what will get my juices flowing. You're worse than an old woman with the way you treat me." He shook his head again to clear his mind. "When you're done, come join me at the table. I need to talk with you."

Larus finished working on the centurion's uniform and then sat at the table and began to eat a bowl of *pulse,* a mash of grains mixed with fat and salt, and a *bucellatum,* a simple biscuit similar to hardtack. "What is it, Gaius Antonius? What is it that can't wait until this evening?"

Gaius finished his breakfast and said, "How long has it been since you were healed? Has it been a year now?"

"Yes, almost a year. That was the last time that we saw Him. Why do you ask?"

"Before I answer that, let me ask you a question. What are they saying on the streets about Yeshua? What is the current opinion on His coming back to the city?"

Larus put his bowl down. "The feeling is that He is the greatest of all the prophets. That's what many of the people are saying. But I have been having my dreams again. They come to me from my tribe. I may be here with you in Judea, but my spirit is still with my people. In my dreams, I have seen who Yeshua is. Do you remember how I followed our gods back in my land? Can you remember how our gods allowed me to heal even you Romans? My gods taught me through my dreams. That is how I learned the healing arts. They came to me on the wind through the trees back in my land, through the rushing waters. Even though they talked to me many times when I was a youth, they stopped talking to me after you captured me. Lately, they have been talking to me again, reminding me of the prophecy that we had back in my land. The prophecy said that the gods would send one down from Heaven who would shepherd His people. It is on the wind, and it is in my dreams; the one who is to shepherd His people is here. Yeshua is the shepherd promised to us. He is not the prophet; He is the Promised One. You know it, too. You felt it when he healed me. Again, why do you ask when it was that He healed me?"

"He'll be here within two days. Do you want to see Him again?"

"Of course I do."

Gaius got up from the table, walked into his room, and began to put on his uniform. Returning to the table, he said, "If He is who you think He is, would you follow Him?" Larus just sat there looking at Gaius. He slowly nodded his head. "Larus, we have been together for what, over thirty years now, correct?" Larus again nodded his head. "Are you familiar with the rules regarding the release of slaves belonging to the Legion?"

"No, I am not. But I am familiar with the rules of war. You captured me fairly; we were defeated on the field of battle, and you had every right to take me."

Gaius continued to put on his uniform. When completely dressed and wearing his distinctive helmet that showed his rank in the Legions, he formally addressed his servant. "Larus, Celtic warrior of the Gallaecian tribes, you who have served me and my family well for many years, you have more than earned your right to walk among free men. As of this day, I am authorized by Roman Law to free you of your bond to me and my century. You are as of this moment a free man. As a token of all that we have endured throughout the years and as my family's affection for you, in addition to your freedom, you are also granted a small offering from my funds to help you as you make your way back into the world of free men. You are welcome to do as you wish, but I believe that I know what you will do, am I right?" Gaius stretched out his hand to Larus.

Larus stood and took Gaius' hand. "How long have you been planning this?"

Gaius smiled. "Since the day that He healed you. You will follow Him, won't you."

"Yes, Gaius Antonius, I will follow Him. And I pray that you will follow Him, too. Let me arrange your affairs first, and I will leave you in two days. I would not be able to forgive myself if I left you in your current disorganized state." He turned to walk into the Centurion's room, but then he stopped and looked back, "Gaius, thank you for this gift, but as I said, you should follow Him, too."

Five days before the Feast of Passover, people all over Jerusalem heard that Jesus was coming to Jerusalem; the news of Lazarus had spread throughout Jerusalem from Bethany, and people wanted to catch a glimpse of this holy man as He entered the city. Declan, Tomy, Ray, Jonathan, and the whole team were on the outskirts of Jerusalem when they heard the crowd's noise at the city gates. Looking over, they could see that Jesus was riding a colt into the city and that people welcomed Him as a victorious general. Declan, seeing this, said to the team, "So, it's true. They welcomed Him into the city as if He were the king. Look at them. They can't contain themselves. Let's head into the city after this crowd thins out. We can't make our way through there right now."

Declan and the rest of the team were observing the crowd and the immediate surroundings. As was typical of a Roman outpost of that time, a century of Roman Legionaries kept an eye on things under the watchful gaze of their centurion on his mount. Declan considered this and told Tomy, "Look at that centurion over there with his troops. He looks to have a pretty good handle on things." He observed the crowd for a moment more, getting a better feel for things. Declan noticed that while most of the crowd was dressed in simple clothes, two men were at the edge of the crowd dressed in fine robes and headdresses; he tucked this information into the back of his mind. "OK, let's see how our cover as a bunch of Greek pilgrims holds out with this guy. Head over there and see if you can learn anything from him about what's happening."

"Got it," Tomy replied. "Let me head over there with Nick and see what we can find out." Tomy made his way with his teammate Nick Stamnas over to where the centurion was mounted on his horse, observing the crowd. As they walked through the crowd towards the Roman troops, Tomy said to Nick, "I'll speak Latin with this guy, and with any luck, he won't speak Greek. I lived in Athens as a kid and speak Greek with an Athenian accent. We're supposed to be from Thessaloniki, and if he speaks Greek, he might pick up my accent."

"Well then, he better not talk to me; I speak Greek with a Connecticut accent," Nick said. "Yeah, take the lead."

Tomy nodded and then asked, "Nick, what are your thoughts so far on all that is happening here?"

"Thoughts? I don't know what to think, but do you want to know how I feel? I feel as if I'm like a drone flying over a movie set. I'm seeing everything, but it's as if I'm detached from everything, like I'm not really here. When I saw who appeared to be Jesus walking through that crowd, my heart almost jumped out of my chest. I could not believe what I was seeing. At my Church back in Waterbury, we have these beautiful icons of Our Lord, and I have to tell you, Jesus didn't look anything like those icons, or should I say the icons don't look anything like Jesus. This is all incredibly strange, but to be honest with you, I am happy to be here. I never thought about being happy on a mission before, excited, yes, but happy? I've never felt like this."

"I hear you," said Tomy. "Do you want to know what else is weird? Looking at these people and hearing how they all speak to each other? If I closed my eyes, I would think I was at home with my extended family. I have this peculiar feeling that I belong here. Enough of my thinking about things; let's go meet this centurion; he looks like he's been around, doesn't he?"

Tomy and Nick carefully approached the Centurion, and then Tomy asked him in Latin, "Begging your pardon, Centurion, but I'm a visitor here and am a bit confused about the ceremony at the city gates. Can you let me know what this excitement is all about?"

The centurion, a bit annoyed by being disturbed from his revelry, was impressed that this pilgrim spoke Latin so well. "Where are you from? You're obviously not from here."

"You're right, Centurion. I am a Greek visiting your beautiful city for my first Passover. My brother and I were wondering who was riding into the city and why He was receiving such a welcome. Is He an official?"

"Well, that explains why you speak our language so well," mused the centurion. "Come, let's go sit over here, and I'll tell you about this man. I've got to get off of this mount anyway. My balls are killing me."

Tomy, Nick, and some of the Roman soldiers followed their centurion into a small, shaded area, the crowd quickly moving out of the centurion's way. When they came to the shaded area, the centurion dismounted, pulled his canteen out, and took a long draught. Several of the Legionaries moved over to where the centurion was sitting. It was almost as if they were guarding him from Tomy and Nick. They must have a reason for doing this, so by a silent agreement, Tomy and Nick were careful not to be perceived as a threat to the centurion. Taking off his plumed helmet and pouring water over his head to clean the dust off, he began talking to Tomy, Nick, and the troops around him. "By the gods, I hate this heat, the flies, this country, everything." He shook the water out of his hair and then looked wistful for a moment. "To be back in Gallaecia, I'd give anything right now to be back home. Oh, yes, let me tell you about this man. He is called 'Yeshua,' and He's a preacher from Nazareth. I was charged to keep the crowd in check today, but my thoughts are, let them honor Yeshua; I know Him, and I like Him. As a matter of fact, I'm surprised that you're even talking to me. You said that this is your first Passover. Are you a new convert to being a Jew?"

Tomy told him, "Yes, my brother and I married Jewesses, so out of respect for them and their family, we became Jews."

The centurion continued, "Well, that explains that too. First your accent, and now your lack of morals." With that, he threw his head back and unleashed a volley of laughter. "You see, you Jews are not supposed to talk to someone like me, a 'Gentile,' because your talking to me would make you unclean. Imagine that, these backward people thinking that Romans would make *them* unclean. That's fine; I can respect their religion and culture. That's what has made Rome so great. We at least respect other people's religions. My century and I have even helped them build their temple. But let me tell you more about this Yeshua. I have this slave; he's more of a servant, well, maybe more than that, and he has been with me for years. He is a Gallaecian, very close to the Cantabrians, one of the many Celtic tribes in northern Hiberia. Hiberia, what some of us now call Hispania, just thinking about the campaigns there makes me shake. It took Rome over two centuries to conquer all of Hiberia. My servant, his name is Larus. We fought his tribes during the Cantabrian Wars, the *Bellum Cantabricum et Asturicum*. If I recall correctly, we started fighting these tribes about sixty years ago. These were the last Celts we fought against in Hiberia after we had conquered all of the Celtiberian tribes in the central part of the province.

"Their country is very mountainous, and the foothills were covered with dense forests of oak, beechwood, and heath. They knew their mountains and forests and took full advantage of their terrain. We arrived in large numbers; I was with the IX Legion, the *Hispana,* and would deploy with our standard formations, which allowed us to defeat all our enemies. Still, they would not engage us directly, at least not regularly. They would attack us quickly and then melt into the mountains or forest. They would attack a column, and we would form up defensively to face them, but as one group would engage our column, another group would attack and destroy our supply columns; it was maddening. They could not defeat us in the field but would destroy our food and water supplies. Imagine how difficult it is to fight in the Hiberian sun all day, only to find that you have no water or food at the end of the fighting. They did a good job of wearing us down. We were always on the defensive, and it took us some time before we could go on the offense against this enemy.

"It was in these mountains and in the foothills that I met Larus on the field of battle. The Cantabri and the Astures were incredible horsemen and foot soldiers. Their foot soldiers excelled in using a short sword, similar to our *gladius.* As a matter of fact, I heard from one of our historians that we actually copied our sword based on the sort of sword that the Celtiberians used against us in Hispania. There may be some truth to that as I know that we have used some of their cavalry tactics. They also wore lightweight leather armor that protected them but gave them unbelievable mobility. They also used a small javelin that they could throw with incredible accuracy. But it was their use of cavalry that almost drove us out of Hiberia.

"The Cantabri horsemen were highly skilled archers who could use bows and arrows or javelins while riding at full speed. Out of nowhere, they would approach our formations in a single file of roughly twenty cavalrymen and then encircle us. Seemingly on command, they would begin to scream, and then they would loose their missiles. They would circle us constantly, all the while shooting and screaming. If it weren't for our order and discipline, we would have fled in fear, but the command *Orbem formate!* would be heard, and we would form our circle. Our archers would fall in behind the front ranks and would provide us with offensive fire. As soon as our archers began to fire, the Cantabri horsemen would withdraw, and then out of their dust, we were set upon by Cantabri foot soldiers.

"The command *Agmen formate!* would be given, and we would assume our square formation. We would hurl our *pila*, our javelins, at the Cantabri. Then our shields would be up, and we would begin to strike the Cantabri with our *gladii*. We would be engaged for a few violent moments and then the Cantabri would disappear back into the mountains.

"But as I was saying about when I met Larus. In the Hibernian campaigns, we usually did not take prisoners; we did not want to let these savages live only to fight us another day. Besides, these Celts would also rather die by suicide instead of being captured and made a slave. We would see many of them killing themselves with their own swords, or they would poison themselves with potions that they kept with them.

"As we were collecting our dead, I noticed that one of the enemy foot soldiers, I did not know if he was *Cantabrian* or *Astures,* was tending to the wounded, not only the Celtic soldiers but Roman Legionaries as well. At that time, I was a young *miles gregarius*, a common foot soldier, although I was the *decanus*, the leader, of our *contubernium*. One of my tentmates pulled out his *gladius* to kill the Celt, but I stopped him as I noticed that the Celt was treating one of our soldiers. This Celt had a basic knowledge of our language, 'My thanks to you, Roman, for sparing me, but I have much work to do to save these men.'

"I told him that I thought that to the *Cantabrians* and *Astures,* dying a soldier's death was considered a victory for them, but the Celt replied, 'If we continue to do that, there won't

116

be any of us left. I am also not of this province; I am from the west, Gallaecia, and a devotee of our god *Endovelicus*, the god of healing. *Endovelicus* does not concern himself under which banner a warrior fights. Healing is meant for us all, just as death comes for us all. Healing and death do not concern themselves with whether you are a Roman or a *Cantabrian*.'

"I asked this Celt as he continued to heal our soldiers and his if he had passed on his art to others of his clan. '*Endovelicus* expects that we share this art with others to honor his name and heal others. I have taught many others this art, but some of my people use this knowledge for evil reasons. Look in my bag.'

"I opened his bag and surmised he used numerous herbs and powders for healing."

'Do you see that purple and red flower?' He pointed to a beautiful little flower; it looked like comfrey. 'Yes, that one. I can use this to stop convulsions and heal wounds, but you can use it as a poison. It can bring death within moments. This is not what *Endovelicus* wants of us. One has to use his art for good, not evil.'

'What is your name, Celt?' I asked him.

'Larus.'

"I then went to find my centurion. I wanted to keep Larus as my slave, and he could be a part of our Century's auxiliary. I found my centurion and approached him. 'Centurion. I have a prisoner that I wish to keep as my personal slave. As *decanus* of my *contubernium,* is that not my right?'

"He answered me, 'Yes, that is your right, but he will be your responsibility. You must feed him out of your own rations, and if he causes any dissent in the ranks or harms any of our Legion, the punishment will be shared by both of you.'

'Thank you, Centurion. He is a healer, and he has healed several of our men in addition to his own. We could use someone like him to teach our physicians the ways of his people as his ways seem very effective in healing.'

"And with that, Larus became my slave. I was prepared to feed and care for him from my own rations, but as I found,

117

the milites gregarii Larus healed were happy to share their rations with him. Larus stayed with me as an auxiliary throughout the rest of the Legion's campaign in the Cantabrian Province, and then we deployed to Gallaecia.

"Larus has served me and our Century well for the past thirty years. He has followed me from Hispania to Rome and to Judea. I recall when we were on patrol east of Jerusalem in the mountains and the surrounding desert of what is called 'The Wilderness.' We were searching for a group of revolutionaries. I believed that they called themselves 'The Zealots,' who were causing significant unrest in Jerusalem. They and a smaller group, the Sicarii, were taking refuge in the Wilderness. By this time, I was a centurion and our century left for the Wilderness on a ten-day patrol. I called my deputy, my optio, over. Marcus Pumidius Rufus was a good man. He had significant experience in the wilderness. 'Marcus Pumidius, which of your men has the best eyes?' I asked him.

'Decimus Ogulnius Barbatus has the eyes of an eagle; he thinks he is a descendent of the Greek goddess Theia.'

'Have Appius Salvinus get him mounted out and ride point. We need sharp eyes ahead of us. These Zealots are known to be able to blend right into the landscape.'

"Our principalis, our senior Legionary, Appius Salvinus Lentulus, sent young Decimus Ogulnius to ride point and two outriders to ride on each of our flanks; having the outriders always made the Legionaries feel better, more optimistic; but on this patrol we had the sense that we were being watched very closely. The century was very quiet. I always took this as a bad sign, but the discipline that was our hallmark kept us moving forward without incident. We kept to the foothills, always trying to maintain the high ground instead of the valleys where the ground was more level but would leave us exposed. In the distance, we could see a small group of men walking slowly across the desert. It may have been my imagination, but it appeared that they were watching us, not us watching them.

"It was a difficult march in the heat of the Wilderness, but the men had enough water and rations, so I was not too concerned. But as the century crested a small hillock, the entire area became incredibly silent. We could not hear any insects buzzing or even any wind. I looked to the west and saw our two outriders, but as I looked east, I could not see our two horsemen. I thought they could have been hidden from view by the rise of the hill to the east.

"Something caught my attention at the top of the small mountain, and I noticed a man lifting something to his mouth. It was the shofar, and before he began to blow his horn signaling the attack, I yelled the command 'Agmen formate!' and the Century immediately formed the square with four smaller lines of soldiers in the middle of the square behind their comrades prepared to launch their pila, the soldiers in the front lines each armed with his shield, his pilum and his gladius, ready to meet the enemy. A large number of Zealots attacked from behind rocks and from over the rise of the hill. They timed their attack perfectly as they charged at us with the sun at their backs and directly in our eyes. We were significantly outnumbered, but our soldiers maintained their discipline and training and solidly held our position. With the second echelon hurling their pila over the heads of their comrades in the first rank and with our soldiers in the first rank using both pila and gladii, the Zealot attack faltered.

"At one point, I looked over the line of the Century and noticed that some of the enemy were falling as if hit by a bolt of lightning. I looked off to the side and noticed Larus with his sling working like a war machine. He was like a catapult, loading and firing, loading and firing, and his aim was more than true for each time he fired his sling, an enemy warrior went down. Here, he was at least sixty years old, and he did not slow down at all. How many of the enemy did he kill? I'll never know, but he was like a young warrior again, and I could not help but smile for him.

"Finally, after possibly one-quarter of an hour, the Zealots withdrew, pulling their dead and wounded with them. I surveyed the field as our soldiers cleared the field of our dead and wounded, and I tried to understand how they could have attacked us without warning. They had possibly used the small group of men in the distance as a ruse to keep our attention focused on them, or it was because they had such a thorough knowledge of the terrain and could move swiftly and silently. I don't know. All that I know is that Decimus Ogulnius Barbatus and our outriders never saw them. That is a lesson we learned through the loss of many Legionaries: when you're in the field searching for them, they are as quiet as the dead of night."

Chapter Twelve

"**But back to your original** question, yes, Larus, he has come to know and believe in this preacher from the wilderness, Yeshua. I had returned to my home in Capernaum, and upon returning, some of my servants met me on the road to tell me that Larus had become very ill. I went in to check on him, and he asked me to send for this preacher. I asked some of the elders in the community to ask for Yeshua. I figured they owed me something, especially after all the work we had done for them, so they went to find Him. Later that day, I was told that Yeshua was on His way to my home. I understand that a Jew cannot come into my home, so I went out to meet Him. Out of respect for Him and for my servant, and also to show this Man whom He was dealing with, I put on my full uniform and dress helmet and met Him a short distance from my home. Again, I respect the religion and traditions of the Jews, plus I care about my servant. He has been like a brother to me and an uncle to my children. For his sake, I wanted this preacher to do what He could to help my servant. I met Yeshua outside. I did not want to offend Him, so I said to Him in Aramaic, 'Thank you for coming.' But then something extraordinary happened. He looked at me with such caring and compassion for my servant and, believe it or not, respect for me. He said to me in Latin, "**Ubi est servus tuus - where is your servant?**" I was told that this was a preacher from the hills, but how could He speak my language so well? I told Him that I know He cannot enter my house, but my servant believes in Him and wants Him to heal him. Understand, I am a Roman centurion. I tell my senior soldiers to do something, and I know that it will be done. So, I asked Yeshua to please help my servant. I straightened up and said to Him in my best grammar and my best Roman accent: 'Domine non sum dignus ut intres sub tectum meum, sed tantum dic verbo et servus curavit: Sir, I am not worthy that you should enter under my roof, but only say the word and my servant shall be healed.' I felt that this Yeshua was more than just a preacher from the wilderness. This was a holy and good man. At that point, I felt like my servant, that this Yeshua was, well, I don't know how to say it, but He was…how can you say…He was different. He looked at the group following Him and said, '**Look at this man. We have the gall to call *him* unclean, but he has more faith, more belief than anyone I have seen in Yisra'eil. Come, let's go to his house, and let us go see his brother.**' He called my servant 'my brother,' how could He know that? It was as if He could read my mind!

"I knew that this would cause a small riot, a rabbi entering the home of a Gentile, so I told Him, 'Sir, as an officer and as one who gives orders, I know that when I tell my soldiers to go do something, I know that it will be done. I know that if You say that my servant will be healed, he will be healed. I know it. I know that whatever You say, it will be done.' He looked at me, and He had a look on His face that I saw in my father when I was young, a look that I can't explain, but it was the same look that my father gave me when I solved something, when I figured something out; that was the same look that He gave me. He put His hand on my shoulder and said, '**You may tell people that I healed your brother, but we both know it was his belief and yours that healed him. Go to him. You will see what your faith and his have done. I give you my Shlama; Pax tecum, do not forget this.**'

"And with that, He left. I stayed there and watched Him and His followers leave. I walked back to my house and walked into my servant's room. When I had left earlier, he was already cold, and there was no life in him, but when I walked back into his room, he was up, talking to everyone and eating. He saw me walk into his room and said, 'I told you, Gaius Antonius Crispinus, that He was a holy man. You know it, too, don't you?' He was right. I know that Yeshua is a holy man, so today, when I saw the crowds flocking to see Him, what was I going to do? Beat the crowd back? I feel like them. He is a holy man; I know that He is. I have served in many places throughout the Empire and seen many things. But I know goodness when I see it. This Yeshua, He is goodness. Does that answer your question?"

Tomy didn't know how to respond. He had all of the knowledge coming from the 21st century of the history of what happened here, plus his faith as a believer in Jesus. Tomy was moved by what the centurion said, but he had to revert back to his role as a Navy SEAL here on a mission. This was becoming harder and harder on Tomy, but he knew what he had to do. He looked at the centurion and said, "Thank you, Centurion. Yes, it does answer my question. But how do you feel? Is this Yeshua more than just another preacher from the provinces?"

"I don't know. I have released Larus and have given him his freedom. He was part of that crowd you saw today, and I'm happy for him. He's following someone who is holy and good. Wouldn't you free your servant to follow someone like Yeshua? If I didn't have to take care of all of these good-for-nothings, I'd follow Him myself!" At this, his troops all shared a laugh and a smile. They loved this old warhorse, and if he said that the preacher from Nazareth was someone they should follow, well then, they'd follow Him.

Tomy and Nick left the company of the Romans and headed back to where Declan and the others were waiting. Tomy reported back to Declan and told him all that he learned. Declan replied, "It's just like it was in Scripture, but you have to hand it to that centurion; he was able to do his duty as a Roman Officer and at the same time realize who Jesus is. OK, we have some time; let's head into the city and keep observing things. We'll talk to some of the locals and see what they know."

Later in the afternoon, the team kept Jesus and His Apostles in view from a distance. They noticed that they had found lodgings near the house of the High Priest Caiaphas. By a stroke of pure luck, the team found lodging relatively close to where Jesus and His Apostles were. Even though the city was crowded because of Passover, they were able to find good lodgings in the Upper City, not too far from Herod's Palace. It must have been the fact that the amount of money that they were given by the Project team back in Pasadena was a small fortune when converted to shekels. The team was settled in comfortably, even Dapples seemed to be enjoying himself. They were able to buy some fresh food, and they enjoyed a nice meal together. Their level of confidence and optimism was buoyed by the fact that they were close to where Jesus was. They felt this would make it easier to observe Jesus and minimize their exposure to the local population. At least, that's what they thought at the time.

After they all ate, Declan and the team sat on cushions at the table and discussed the day's events and what their plan was going to be moving forward. Declan started the meeting off, "I wanted to go over a few things while we're settled in, and things are a bit quiet after this morning's events in Bethany. Before we get started, does anyone have anything pressing to bring up?"

Sam Odeh, one of the SEALs who was a member of Ray's group, asked, "Any word from Michael's team?"

"Not yet. I think they got misrouted during the transit, and they're either delayed in getting to us, or they never left the present time, and they're still on the pad. Just know that all of us team leaders, Michael, Tomy, Ray, and I, were given specific instructions on what to do if this contingency popped up, so they should be good to go. We left them a marker and instructions on where to go when they finally get here so they could join up when they can. In the meantime, all four of our teams are deployed with the same equipment. We're all self-contained, so Michael and his guys have what they need to keep them going. Good question, anyone else?"

"Yeah, Deck, Earlier you mentioned equipment and that we may have lost some of our gear. How are we holding out with our supplies, especially ammo?" asked Josh Romano, the Air Force PJ from Declan's fire team.

"OK, we lost two ammo boxes in transit, you all know that. But each of us carried a good supply, and I had a small box in my dune-buggy. Luckily, all our smoke cans and flash-bangs made it through, so we're pretty well set. We're all supposed to be good at staying invisible, so let's continue keeping off the skyline. I don't think we'll have to worry too much about using our firepower."

Tomy jumped in, "famous last words. The centurion we talked to mentioned that the Zealots are still causing some problems. We need to give those guys a wide berth."

"Speaking of which," said Declan, "do you want to give the guys a quick update on what the centurion told you and Nick?"

"Absolutely. The good news is that he bought our story about us being Greek pilgrims. The bad news is that since we talked with him, he knows we're here and may keep an eye on us. He's no dummy, and he's been around the block a few times. He's as wary as a cat. It's like in Scripture, though. He told us about his approaching Jesus and asking Him to heal his servant. He's pretty devoted to his servant, too. They've been through some stuff together."

"Did he comment about your accent? Was he suspicious about anything?" Declan asked Tomy and Nick.

"Not really. Tomy told them he and I were brothers on a pilgrimage from Greece. I think he was surprised that Tomy spoke Latin so well," said Nick. "This is just me talking, but I think that although he may have met us, with all the pilgrims in Jerusalem right now, I don't know if he'll give Tomy or me a second thought. Tomy may be right, but I think he's more concerned about retirement."

Tomy thought about this, "Yeah, you're probably right. I may be overthinking this, but as Deck said, we'll just maintain our low profile and keep blending in. How's that sound to everyone?"

"Sounds good to me. Thanks, guys, for the input. OK,

let's review our plans for the rest of the week," Declan started back up. "According to the calculations from the guys in Pasadena, the portal should reopen in another week, so we have six more days until we head back to the Central Mountains. With the time that we have, we'll continue to observe Jesus of Nazareth and record anything of interest that you may see. By tomorrow morning, we'll have our assigned areas designated for where we'll be surveilling our subject. After our training in Jerusalem West, we should all have a fairly good idea of the layout of this city and where our rally points will be. Jerry has a watch schedule put together for while we're here in this house, any questions?"

"Deck, can we talk about what we saw today in Bethany?" Kahlil "Kelly" Sabbagh brought this up. "What we saw with Lazarus and his sisters, was anyone else as freaked out as much as I am about what we saw today? I mean, I'm Lebanese, and I'm used to seeing families at funerals wail and scream; that's no big deal, but what we saw today...Deck, how can I not call it like I see it? What was our mission, 'to observe Jesus of Nazareth?' Guys, I observed things today that must be reported."

"I hear you, Kelly. Tomy and I talked about this today. We're going to be writing an after-action report, and we're all going to corroborate all that we saw; that's our mission: observe and report. As I mentioned earlier, each one of us will be recording anything that we see. We'll take all of our reports, compile everything, and add this to our after-action report. Guys, just do what we always do when we're gathering intel. Nothing should escape our attention. Now, I need to say something. A lot of us on this team are believers in Jesus of Nazareth. I'm going to try to be completely objective and put my personal religious beliefs aside for a moment. At this time, it appears that what has been recorded in the Christian Gospels is, from a purely historical perspective, true. That being said, we all know how this will play out. As Christians, we know that Jesus is going to suffer a horrible death, but as believers, we know why. There is nothing that we can do to change any of this, and as per our orders, we are not allowed to interfere with anything that is going to happen. Are we all clear on this?"

Everyone nodded their assent.

"OK, then we're set. Keep recording all of your observations and gather as much intel as possible. We're only several days away from returning to our time, so let's stick to what we do best. One last thing: remember that we have to try to find some artifacts or other proof that we made it here. I got some local currency, and the coins are all in perfect condition. That's an example of what we can take back; keep an eye out for some stuff. There will be lots of merchants out here selling their wares for Passover; that might be a good place to look, OK? Any other questions or comments?"

"Yeah, Deck," Kelly Sabbagh asked. "Would it be OK to bring back some weapons, like a knife or something? I'm sure that some of these merchants out there would be selling knives and such. Are you OK with that?"

"Sure, these folks always had to have a knife with them as one of their main tools to take with them when they were out in the fields. Look at something like that, or even a farm implement or something. Those things have to have archeological value, and they'll prove that we were here. Good stuff, anyone else?"

"Deck, I need to get something off my chest," Jonathan added. "Do you recall when we were all at Lazarus' home, and the Rabbi was walking away? The Rabbi kept looking back at Lazarus. He was smiling at His friend, but Deck, as the Rabbi looked back over His shoulder, He glanced away from Lazarus and looked right at me. He more than looked at me. He *looked* at me, and I could swear He was talking to me. I'm a pretty level-headed Marine and try to be as rational as the next guy, but when the Rabbi looked at me, it was as if He were looking into the depths of my soul. I'm not trying to be dramatic, it's…it's…it's too hard to explain. Something happened back there, and it's as if…Let me tell you guys something, and this is no shit. I was a young Marine getting ready to pump out with a MEU, and we were loading all of our gear onto the ship at the pier. There were these Port-a-Johns lined up across from the ship on the other side of the pier, and I went into one of them to take a dump. Some young Marine from Landing Support was operating this crane and lifting this big ISO container, but he lost the load. This ISO container drops on that line of Port-a-Johns, and it drops directly across the front side of these shitters. Can you believe this? There wasn't one single Marine using those Port-a-Johns; it was just me having a seat in the very last one. If I had been standing up and taking a leak, I would have been crushed, but since I was sitting on the pot, it missed me by about three inches. Here I am, minding my own business, and the next thing I know, this huge ISO container is dropped right in front of me. If I had been constipated before I got in there, that ISO container would have taken care of that. Afterward, I guess I went into shock, but the split second after that container invaded my personal space, I had this feeling that I just escaped death. That's the feeling I had when the Rabbi looked at me."

The team was stunned at this story, and then they all, Jonathan included, exploded with laughter. Ray Boutros got up and said, "Jonathan, I have never heard anyone explain a near-death experience like that. You are one funny Jarhead, Bro!"

Then Tomy spoke up, "I hear what Jonathan is saying. He's right. Jonathan, He looked at you and saw into your soul because He has something planned for you."

The rest of the evening was spent checking their equipment and just talking with each other. As was the custom of the time, the house they were living in had a courtyard, and on the south side of the courtyard was a small, covered area that was Dapples' home for the night. Jerry DiCenzo had a watch bill drawn up and took the first watch of the night.

The following day, as Declan, Tomy, and Jonathan were walking through the city gathering intel, Declan noticed the two men from the crowd he had seen yesterday. He motioned Tomy and Jonathan to follow his lead as he approached the two men. Speaking in Aramaic, he said to them, "*Shlama* and good morning, Gentlemen. My brothers and I are pilgrims from

Thessaloniki, and we saw you yesterday at the City Gates. We all saw a high-ranking official being welcomed into the city. Is there a chance that you might tell us who that official was?"

Both men stared at Declan with apprehensive looks, but they did not answer him.

Declan looked at them with a puzzled look and thought that the men did not understand him. "My apologies, gentlemen. It appears that maybe you did not understand me. My brother is more fluent in your language than I am."

Tomy took over. "I am sorry, but my brother does not speak your language well. We are pilgrims visiting Jerusalem for our first Passover, and we are unfamiliar with some of your customs and the things happening in your city at this time. We saw that official being welcomed into the city and were just curious if he was someone we should know. Might we ask if you know that man? He did appear to be very respected and admired by the crowd."

One of the men replied, "So, you are here for your first Passover. You have never been here before?"

"No, sir, we have never been here. We are recent converts to the faith of Father Abraham, and we are fulfilling our obligation to make a pilgrimage to Jerusalem for the Feast of Passover."

The other man replied, "Well, that's commendable, but we are on our way to do our obligation according to the Law. We are working to help the outcasts of our society; we wish you a good day." Both men turned and began to walk away.

Tomy reached out and touched one of the men on the shoulder, "Is there a way that we can help you? We could learn more about the Law from you if we help."

The men looked at each other, and the first one replied, "Meet us back here at midday, and we will see if you can assist us." They walked away, and the first one said, "I don't know, Joseph. They might be from the Council trying to incriminate us. Let's see if they return here at noon and if they wish to help. I doubt that anyone from the Council would want to work with lepers. It may be that they're pilgrims from Thessaloniki."

Joseph replied, "Nicodemus, we have been able to avoid suspicion because we have been careful. We should proceed with caution."

*****

At midday, Declan, Tomy, and Jonathan returned to where Joseph and Nicodemus told them to meet them. They waited for about fifteen minutes, and then Joseph and Nicodemus arrived.

Joseph said, "So, you did want to help. Good, but be careful what you ask for. We will be working to provide food for a colony of lepers living in an area not far from here." He was surprised that none of the pilgrims flinched upon hearing they would be working with lepers.

Tomy replied, "Two of the members in our group are trained in the healing arts. Would you like their help as well?"

Joseph answered, "Yes, they would be welcome to help. You will find the Water Gate on the south side of the city. Leave by that gate and walk to the southeast for an hour. You will be met by one of our servants who will take you to the place of the lepers. Now go, we will see you there." Joseph and Nicodemus walked away.

Declan said, "Let's get Josh and Sam and head out there. We have to get a move on; let's go." They caught up with the rest of the team and told them where they were headed. Josh and Sam joined Declan, Tomy, and Jonathan and left the City.

As they were told, a servant was waiting for them on the trail. They followed the servant into an old, unused rock quarry honeycombed with many caves. Tomy asked, "I know that we got all of our inoculations back in Warner Springs before we left, but I don't think we got immunized against leprosy, did we?"

Sam answered, "Don't worry, Tomy, we'll be fine, and just for the record, it's Hansen's Disease. It might be an infectious disease, but it's not very contagious. If this really spooks you, don't get too close to the patients. Our immune systems are strong, and we're well nourished, so we should be OK. We would have to be exposed to the people for a long period of time before we become 'at risk,' follow my and Josh's lead, and watch what we do. If it makes you feel more comfortable, go ahead and pull your head covering over your mouth and nose. Just know you can shake their hands and sit with them at a table without being affected. "

Jonathan asked, "What are we going to do here? We can't treat these lepers as if we're back home, can we? This raises another question: if we treat these people with modern medicine, isn't that going against our primary directive? I mean, we're interfering with things here."

Josh chimed in, "No to both of our questions. First off, we're not treating these people with modern medicine. We have a drug regimen back home; what is it, Sam, Dapsone, Rifampin, and something else, I can't remember, that is used to treat Hansen's? We don't have anything like that here. But we can do other things for these patients without treating them with modern drugs."

"You're right, and I think the other drug was clofazimine, something like that. I can't remember either," Sam answered. "But as Josh was saying, we can treat some of their other problems like teaching them to keep their wounds clean. I think that if we focus on basic hygiene and making sure that they're drinking clean water, that will help them. Look, we can't cure any of these people here, but we can help them get stronger. That will do a lot to keep the bug that causes Hansen's Disease at bay. We can also help them to be more comfortable and enjoy what they have left of their lives. Lastly, we know that many people with Hansen's Disease overcome their disease naturally. We're just helping them improve their health."

They walked down into the quarry, where they were met by a man who was helping bring food down to the quarry floor. They saw some people who looked like ghosts moving around in the caves. They hesitated to leave their caves until the man with the food called them all out. The shadowy figures began to come out into the sunshine. Before they came out, they all began to ring their bells and shout, "Unclean! Unclean!"

Tomy looked up at the top of the quarry and saw the two well-dressed figures from Jerusalem looking down at all of them. He asked the man with the food, "We're here to help you, my friend, but tell me, how you are called?"

"I am called Jehial, and I thank you for your help. I was told that you also have a physician with you. Is that correct?

"Yes, it is, Jehial. I have another question: do you know those two men standing over there? We told them we would like to help here but do not even know who they are."

"Ah, that is Nicodemus and Joseph. They are both well-respected members of Jerusalem. Nicodemus is a Pharisee and a member of the Sanhedrin, and Joseph is a member of the Council. They have been very generous with their time and money in helping these lepers."

Declan asked, "And what is your role here, Jehial? Are you also a member of the Council?"

At that last remark, Jehial laughed, "Not at all. No, I used to be a member of this community; I had lived here for many years, and then one day, a number of us were begging in the village, and then we saw the Master. We all begged Him to have pity on us and hopefully give us some money, but He didn't give us any money. No, He cleansed us. He told me that it was my faith that saved me. So, that's what I am doing here; I am letting everyone know that their faith can save them. Maybe not cleanse them as I was, but save them so they may enter the Kingdom of God. But enough of me, come, let us help these people."

The team helped deliver food to everyone, and Josh and Sam had a chance to treat a number of the people who were there. "You have to make sure that these patients do what they can to keep their wounds clean," Josh told Jehial. "Make sure they keep them washed and then covered with a clean cloth. This will help prevent their wounds from getting worse."

Sam worked with Jehial to make sure that the community kept their water clean. Their water jugs were full of water mixed in with dirt and debris, and he showed him how to make an improvised water purification system. Sam brought everyone over to him and showed Jehial what to do. "Take your large water jugs and let them sit out overnight. This will allow most of the dirt to settle at the bottom. Then, get another large water jug that is clean. Get a clean cloth and put some rocks and pebbles on this cloth, then fold it so that it is like a small purse full of coins. Then, hold this purse over the opening of the clean jug and open the purse up. Have someone pour the water from the jug that was left out overnight and over the cloth into the other jug; this will clean the water. After that, hang this jug over your cooking fire until it boils. Do this from now on; your water will be cleaner, and it will help you."

Josh and Sam told Jehial to make sure that they kept their clothes washed on a regular basis. "You must teach them to keep themselves and their clothes clean," Josh said. "What kind of food do you get them?"

"We bring them bread, lentils, and some meat on occasion. What else should I bring them?"

"See if you can bring them some fruit. I know there are pomegranates, dates, figs, grapes, and other fruits here. Try to bring them as many fruits as possible."

The team worked with Jehial and his community for the rest of the day, and then they made their way out of the quarry. When they reached the top, Joseph and Nicodemus were waiting for them. Joseph welcomed them, "Thank you for what you did for these outcasts of our society, but aren't you afraid of them?"

Tomy spoke for the group, "We have seen many things back in our home country and in our travels. Not once have we been affected by any sickness we have seen."

"Then God, and Blessed be His Name, must have His mark on you. Let us walk back to the city with you." They began to walk back toward Jerusalem. "We haven't told you who we are. I am called Joseph, and I am from Arimathea. My colleague is Nicodemus, a prominent Jerusalem citizen. We welcome you all to Jerusalem. Now, what questions do we have for us."

Declan said, "We met Jehial down by the caves. He told us that he was a member of this community until he was healed of his disease by someone he called 'The Master.' Do you know of whom he was speaking?"

Nicodemus smiled at Joseph and then at Declan. "The Master. That was the man you saw riding into the city, the Man you thought was one of our officials. He is not an official of the city, or any city for that matter. He is a very holy and learned Rabbi from the north. He is called Yeshua, and it is reported that He has performed many miracles."

"What do you think? Has He performed any miracles? If he indeed cleansed Jehial, that is something that I would like to investigate."

Joseph picked up from there, "There have been many people who have seen Yeshua perform many unexplainable things. We don't know if they are true, but His message is fascinating, and He has many people who follow Him."

Tomy asked, "Are you and Nicodemus His followers?"

Joseph looked pensive and then answered, "We follow The Law, but many preachers from the wilderness claim to be prophets, and this Yeshua may be one of them. As I said, though, His message is intriguing, and I think that we are more 'interested' instead of being followers."

Declan said, "In Greece, we have many scholars who predict that one will be sent down from Heaven to save his people. This person is called the Anointed One, the Christ. Do you feel that this Yeshua may be the Christ?"

Nicodemus stopped and looked at Declan sharply, "What would make you say that? He is a preacher from the north who speaks an interesting message. He is nothing more than that." He turned on his heel and continued walking at a faster pace toward Jerusalem. Joseph ran to catch up with him.

Tomy touched Declan on the shoulder, "Why did you say that? You know that both Joseph and Nicodemus are secret followers of Jesus, but they're being very quiet about it because of fear of the Sanhedrin, or as Scripture tells us, 'for fear of the Jews.' You almost blew it, Deck; we know who Jesus is because of where we're from; we can't give that away."

"Sorry, Tomy, it just came out. Let's catch up with

them, and let me see if I can smooth things over."

Joseph caught up with Nicodemus, "What is wrong? We don't need to be rude to these men."

"I don't know if I trust them. It sounded like he was trying to trick me into saying we know who the Master is. They might be working for Caiaphas."

"You don't believe that, do you? After what we saw those men do with the lepers, no one associated with Caiaphas would do anything like that. They might be exactly who they say they are, new converts to our faith.."

Nicodemus appeared to calm down as Declan and the rest caught up to them. Declan approached Nicodemus, "Sir, I am sorry if I said anything to offend you. As we said earlier, we want to learn more about our faith."

"No, I apologize to you for my rudeness. Let's walk together and we will gladly share with you more about the Law and the faith of Abraham. In three days, we will celebrate one of our highest Holy Days when we celebrate our deliverance out of Egypt..."

It was a stimulating walk back to the city. The entire team spent the following two days helping Joseph and Nicodemus with the community of lepers and the poor throughout the city. They also learned from their many dealings with the people that many believed that Yeshua was not only a teacher but that He was the promised Messiah who had come to deliver His people.

Chapter Thirteen

Passover in Jerusalem, 33 A.D.

The next morning, the three fire teams had their designated areas for observation assigned. The plan was that each unit would have a specific area assigned for two hours and then rotate with another section. In this manner, if the team members were observed, the same faces would not be seen for too long in one area. The teams would be able to maintain contact via their two-way radios at designated times in which they were to check in with each other and schedule their rotations; emergency calls were to be made as needed.

For the first watch of the day, Declan's fire team of Jonathan, Kevin, and Josh were assigned to patrol and observe the area in the southern part of the Upper City. This was not too far from where they were lodging, with the Palace of Herod designated as the center of their assigned section. This patrol section allowed Deck's team to keep the Upper Room, where Jesus was under close observation. They planned to ensure that a team could monitor the Upper Room uninterruptedly.

Tomy's fire team, Nick, Jerry, and Kelly, was assigned the area from the Judgment Gate to the Sheep Gate, which allowed them to keep the Antonia Fortress and Pilate's Palace under observation. The center of this patrol section was the Sheep Gate, which was directly south of the Antonia Fortress.

Ray's fire team, John, Antoine, and Sam, was to patrol the area from the Golden Gate to the Royal Portico, allowing them to keep the temple under observation. The center of this

136

patrol section was the Royal Portico, which was very close to the main entrance to Temple Mount.

Heading north by northeast, it was approximately 1,000 meters from the Palace of Herod to the Judgment Gate. Heading directly south, it was 1,000 meters from the Palace of Herod to the House of Caiaphas, close to the Upper Room. Heading northeast, it was 1,000 meters from the Judgment Gate to the Antonia Fortress and the Sheep Gate. Heading due south, it was 1,000 meters from the Sheep Gate to the Royal Portico, and heading southwest, it was 1,500 meters from the Royal Portico to the House of Caiaphas. The three fire teams could move clockwise and complete a circuit around the central part of the Old City of Jerusalem.

To keep their assigned sectors under surveillance, two of the members from each fire team would head over to their next assigned sector to relieve the team currently in that area; once properly relieved, the two remaining members would join the other group in the new sector. In this manner, surveillance was constant.

The team kept this surveillance up from 7:00 in the morning until 7:00 in the evening, and then they would return to their temporary house. In the days before electricity, most people would return home at sunset and be in bed after their evening meal. It would be unusual to be out in the streets too long after sunset, as that would raise suspicion, so the plan was to act the same way as the local population. The main team would retire to the house and a small team of two would continue to make rounds for a few more hours after sunset. As special operators, they could make their patrols undetected. The only thing they could report after several nights of observing the Upper Room was that Jesus and His followers would stay in their room and talk for most of the evening. It sounded as if Jesus was simply teaching His Apostles about the Kingdom of God.

*****

The team had been very cautious but executed perfectly

what they were all trained to do. They shadowed Jesus and His followers during the time leading up to the Passover celebration and observed all they were doing without their being noticed. For the Passover Seder, many families stayed awake well past their usual bedtime and celebrated as a family. It was a warm, pleasant night, and everyone had their shutters open. You could hear from the street the family celebrations that were taking place. Jonathan and Jerry had the evening patrol and watched all of this. As he saw and listened to what was occurring in people's homes, Jonathan was overwhelmed by the solemnity of the celebrations, and he began to understand fully what this meant to him as a Jew and what it meant to his people. His Jewishness began to overtake him. The memories of the Seder meals he had shared with his family and extended family returned to him, and he began to yearn for those days. The sight of families gathering to celebrate their deliverance from the Pharaoh, the smell of the food cooking, and everything began to overwhelm him. He was a Jew, his father was a Jew, and his mother was a Jew, and at that point, he became ashamed of himself for abandoning his faith. Thousands of years of history could not be erased from his soul. He finally understood what God wanted of him. Like Tomy, he realized that these were his people. Like a torrent rising up from within him, the Shema was burning in his heart. He covered his eyes with his right hand, and he began to pray the prayer of all Jews:

Sh'ma Yisra'eil Adonai Eloheinu Adonai Echad!
(Then whispering, he said,)
Baruch shem k'vod malkhato le'olam va'ed.
V'ahav'ta eit Adonai Elohekha m'odekha
b'khol l'vav'kha uv'khol naf'sh'kha.
uv'khol m'odekha

Hear o Israel, the Lord is our God, the Lord is One!
Blessed be the Name of His glorious Kingdom forever and ever, and you shall love the Lord your God, With all of your heart and with all of your soul, and with all of your might.

Jonathan knew in his mind what he was here to do, but in his heart and soul, he knew now who he was and what God expected of him.

Jerry was watching his teammate, Jonathan. "Hey, Bro, are you doing all right? Looks like you're spacing out on me a bit."

"No, it's just all that I'm seeing right now. This is bringing back a lot of memories of my family. We held Seders as a kid growing up with all of my family: grandparents, uncles, aunts, everyone. Seeing this here and hearing the same words spoken at the table, it's just lots of memories flooding back to me, and I'm ashamed that I abandoned my faith. At our family Seder, we had fourteen steps taken for our ceremony, from the blessing of the wine to the end. We would recite the *Haggadah,* the telling of our first Passover when the Angel of The Lord would Pass Over our homes and spare our first-born sons. I was the youngest in our house for many Seders, so I would ask the four questions. I can still recite the first question: *Ma nishtanah halailah hazeh mikol haleilot?* Why is this night different from all other nights? It was amazing. We ate bitter herbs in our house; it was normally horseradish to remind us of our bitter time in captivity. It's difficult to explain, but I miss it beyond belief right now."

"I hear you. I grew up in a huge Sicilian family, a bunch of ginzos we were. We'd have these parties for Christmas and New Year's, *minchia,* talk about food, we'd eat for days, *mangia, mangia, mangia.* Yeah, but when you look back at it, it's the fact that we were all together that made those family get-togethers so good. I remember this one Christmas that we had my *Nonno, Noninna and even my Bisnonna, you know, my grandparents and my great-grandmother, all at the house; those* are great memories, so I know what you're feeling, like being homesick.."

"Yeah, but Jerry, you're a Catholic, right? Did you abandon your faith?"

"Nah, I make Mass on Easter and Christmas, maybe an occasional wedding for friends and family, or I'll make a funeral Mass if someone croaks, but I never really left the Church."

"That's the difference between us. I did, and I feel sick about it," Jonathan said. "Look around at what we're seeing out here or what we saw in Bethany. Doesn't this make you think that the religions we're practicing aren't just something that we do because of our family background or our culture? Don't you think that this proves there's something more to religion than that?"

Jerry was very quiet and then looked at Jonathan, "After what we have seen here, you'd have to have *stronzo* for brains if you couldn't figure out that there is a God in Heaven. Yeah, I'll have to level with you. I feel terrible about not attending Mass as often as I should. Especially with the shit that we've been through every time we head down range, I need to pull my head out. Thanks, Jonathan, I feel totally miserable now."

They both laughed and then Jonathan said, "Actually, I feel better now; hey, let's get back to where the Rabbi and His followers are; let's see what's up." With that, they continued with their rounds.

They walked past the house of Caiaphas towards where Jesus and His Apostles were holding their Seder. They heard the men singing songs; hearing them sing *"Hoshiya Na"* brought back more memories for Jonathan; after thirty minutes, they noticed one of the Apostles had left the house and ran toward the temple. Jerry knew what was going on, so he called Declan to report that things would start happening fairly quickly.

Declan directed Jerry and Jonathan to keep a visual on the Apostle while he deployed the rest of the teams to their assigned positions. Tomy's fire team of Nick and Kelly headed towards the main entrance of the Temple Mount. Jerry would join up with his team once they arrived. Declan then deployed his fire team members Kevin and Josh to maintain observation of the Upper Room by the House of Caiaphas and have Jonathan meet up with the two of them. Declan was going to stay in the house and direct activities from there. Ray's fire team of John, Antoine, and Sam deployed towards the Horse Gate, immediately due west of the Temple. Declan knew this would give Ray's section quick access to the Garden of Gethsemane.

The plan was to split Tomy's and Ray's teams at an appropriate time on Declan's order to provide additional coverage to Herod's Palace and the Antonia Fortress. Within thirty minutes, they had all three areas under observation; all was quiet.

They all knew what was transpiring, but they continued to observe. A short while later, Kevin, Jonathan, and Josh reported to Declan that Jesus and two or three of His followers also left the house and were walking towards a wooded area on the outskirts of the neighborhood, towards the Garden of Gethsemane. Declan had Ray deploy Antoine and Sam to observe the Garden area while Ray and John kept watch at the Horse Gate.

Later in the evening, Antoine and Sam reported from the wooded area where Jesus was praying with His followers that a group of armed Temple guards had arrested Jesus. A fight had taken place with one of Jesus' followers, who drew a sword and cut off someone's ear; they could not tell who it was. But Jesus had told His follower to put the sword away, and He told him, **"Do you not think that I can call upon My Father, and He will not provide Me with more than twelve legions of angels?"** Antoine then reported to Declan that it looked as if the guards were taking Jesus away and were heading south towards where Kevin, Jonathan, and Josh were. Declan had Antoine and Sam continue to shadow Jesus and the guards that had taken Him. Declan began moving the various fire teams around: Kevin, Jonathan, and Josh would move a couple hundred yards to the west and observe what they could at Caiaphas' house. Antoine and Sam were following Jesus; Ray and John would move to the north towards the Sheep Gate as this was close to Pilate's palace; Tomy and Nick would move 2,000 yards to the west towards Herod's palace while Jerry and Kelly would move north towards the staircases that led to the Antonia Fortress. Everyone waited to hear what Antoine, Sam, Kevin, and Josh would report.

*****

Caiaphas' House

Kevin and Josh reported that Jesus was taken to the house of the High Priest, Caiaphas. Then, Antoine and Sam reported that some of Jesus' followers had stopped a distance from the High Priest's house and were sitting by a campfire in a small courtyard; they appeared to be confused and very anxious. One of the followers, who was bigger than the rest of them, got into an argument with two of the women who were there in the courtyard. The discussion got very heated, and then the follower shook his head in disgust and then ran out of the courtyard; at that moment, a rooster crowed, and it looked as if the follower fell down and crumpled in grief.

"That must be St. Peter," said Sam. "It's true; he must have been denying Jesus to those women. He looks completely lost right now; look at him!" Inside Caiaphas' house, Kevin reported that it looked as if a group of religious leaders was interrogating Jesus in a large hall, and from the looks of things, it did not appear to be going too well for Him. He was being screamed at by the group of officials, and some were beginning to abuse Him physically. After some time, the guards took Him out of the main hall and into another area of the house. Kevin and Josh lost sight of him and it appeared that things were done for the night. Antoine and Sam checked back in and reported that Jesus' followers had all fled the area and were nowhere to be found. It did not appear as if they had returned to their Upper Room. The teams kept a watch of their respective areas, and towards the end of the night, they all rallied back to their house to wait for the morning.

Before dawn the following morning, Declan deployed the teams in the same areas they were in the night before. They understood that today would be very fluid and fast-moving. Kevin, Jonathan, and Josh took up station outside of Caiaphas' house and reported to Declan that Jesus had been bound and was being led away by the guards and heading north. Josh could pick up some chatter from the crowd following the guards that Jesus was being taken to Pilate's Judgment Hall.

"Got it, Josh. Let me get a hold of Ray and John and have them stand by. In the meantime, fall behind the crowd and keep me updated as to what's going on." Declan then contacted Jerry and Kelly, who were close to the Antonia Fortress.

"Jerry and Kelly, you have a group of guards escorting Jesus to Pilate's Hall. Ray and John are going to be moving toward your way." Declan contacted Ray and John to update them.

"Ray and John, you have a group heading your way; they're bringing Jesus to Pilate's Hall, and Jerry and Kelly will be in the area directly. Kevin, Jonathan, and Josh will continue trailing the crowd heading your way."

Declan then updated Tomy and Nick and told them to stay where they were outside of Herod's Palace until Declan could join up with them. Declan wanted to be with Tomy and Nick. They would also trail the crowd so that they could be at the Prefect's palace when Jesus was before Pilate.

Pilate's Headquarters

As the Chief Priests and the Elders delivered the bound Jesus to Pilate for judgment, it became apparent that Pilate was not pleased that they brought an issue to him that they could have dealt with themselves. The Chief Priests and Elders then explained to the Prefect that since today was one of their major holy days, they could not pass judgment during that time. This issue needed to be addressed immediately. Time was of the essence. Pilate returned to his residence in the Praetorium. He couldn't think with all of the noise and bickering that was occurring in his hall.

Pilate was sitting in his solarium when his wife approached him. His wife, Claudia Procula, was a very wealthy noblewoman, and like many other noblewomen of the day, she was very well educated. She had traveled with Pilate throughout Judea and provided him with good counsel.

"I sent a message to you earlier this morning, but I do not know if your servant delivered it to you. Are you involved

143

with this matter of the Teacher from Nazareth?"

"I did not receive your message, Claudia, and yes, I am involved with this issue," answered her husband.

"Why are you getting involved? Isn't this a religious matter for Caiaphas and his gang of tongue waggers? Why have they involved you with this?"

Pilate let out a long breath in frustration and resignation. "They're telling me that they have a very pressing matter with this Man, and because it is one of their high holy days, they are prohibited from working, as they told me, 'They can't pass judgment.' After all of these years dealing with these temple priests, I have the suspicion that every day must be a holy day for them, they never work."

"Marcus, listen to me. I heard what these priests were saying, and I am very concerned about your involvement with this Jesus of Nazareth. I was troubled deeply by a dream that I had. In my dream, it was revealed to me that this is a righteous man and that any dealings you have with him will not turn out well for you. Why don't you release him?"

Pilate looked at his wife with affection. "You and your dreams. I have listened to you many times when it comes to your dreams; for the most part, they have been somewhat foretelling. Let me talk with these people and see what can be done."

"Be cautious, Marcus. Caiaphas and his cohort are as pestilent as the snakes and scorpions of the Judean desert."

"Claudia," Pilate assured his wife. "You know how cautious I can be. You appear to be the only one defending this Man. Why is that? Is it only because of your dreams?"

"It's not only my dream, but I have heard several of our servants speaking of Him. By all accounts, He is a righteous Man who speaks of love and forgiveness, and combined with what I know of Caiaphas, I hold more credence in what the servants say than that braying donkey."

This struck Pilate as interesting that Claudia had the same opinion of Caiaphas as he did. "What have you heard of Caiaphas? What do you know of his actions?"

Smiling at her husband, Claudia answered, "I have my

spies, too, my beloved."

"He is just a simple preacher from Nazareth who appears to be upsetting the Temple Priests. From what I understand, he is illiterate and very common. Let me see how well my Aramaic can hold out so that I can question this Man."

Claudia warned her husband again, "Proceed with caution, Marcus. I have a feeling about this Man, and you know that my dreams have served you well in the past."

"Yes, my dear." Shaking his head in amusement, Pilate then went out into the courtyard where they had Jesus waiting. Although Pilate dismissed what Claudia said, what she said intrigued him.

****

Tomy, Nick, and Declan blended in with the crowd in the pavement area outside the Roman Prefect's Palace. The Chief Priests could not enter Pilate's Praetorium as they would be defiled, so Pilate held discussions with the Chief Priests and the elders in this outside area, commonly called the *Gabbatha*. Pilate's servants brought Pilate's judgment seat outside. As Tomy, Nick, and Declan were much closer to the wall of the Praetorium's courtyard, they could hear all that Pilate and the Chief Priests were saying. The crowd was being agitated by members of the Temple guards who were mingling with the crowd.

Pilate wanted to speak with Jesus directly, so he exited the Praetorium and summoned Jesus. Pilate's Aramaic was rudimentary at best, and he wanted to ask Jesus if he were the "King of the Jews," as Caiaphas accused him. As Pilate struggled to speak yet still maintain a modicum of the dignity of his position, Jesus answered in flawless, aristocratic Latin, **"ego facillime possunt loqui latine, si ita volunt - I can very easily speak Latin if you so wish."** This greatly surprised Pilate as he could not believe that a common preacher from the hinterlands could speak Latin. This made him recall what his wife had said to him regarding his not getting involved with this righteous man, and he began to reevaluate his initial dismissal of his wife's admonition.

Pilate then spoke again to the Chief Priests and asked them what the specific charges were against this man. They began to tell Pilate, "He has been misleading our people, telling them that He opposes paying taxes to Caesar. He has even said that He is a king, the king of the Jews. We have no king but Caesar!" Pilate approached Jesus and asked Him, "Do you hear what they are saying about You? Are You the King of the Jews?"

Jesus replied, **"Est tibi, qui dicit, ego sum. Hoc est aliquid, quod te, dicens, in tua, vel quod est hoc aliquid quod dico vobis? - It is you who says that I am. Is this something that you are saying on your own, or is this something that they are telling you?"**

Pilate said to Him, "It's not me who is accusing You; it's your own people, your own priests! They are saying this, they have handed You over to me. What have You done? Are you the King of the Jews?"

Jesus answered him "**Regnum meum non est de hoc mundo. Quod si verum esset, non tibi videtur quod mea comites esset pugna ad custodiam me ab esse tradita ad Iudaeos enim poena? - My kingdom is not of this world. If it were, don't you think that my attendants would be fighting to keep me from being handed over to the Jews for punishment?"**

Pilate said, "So you are a King?"

And Jesus answered, "**iterum, est qui dicit, ego sum. Sed ad hoc quod natus sum et ad hoc veni in mundum, ut testimonium perhibent Veritati. Omnis, qui pertinet ad veritatem audit vocem Meam. - again, it is you who says that I am. But it was for this that I was born, and for this, I came into the world to testify to the Truth. Everyone who belongs to the truth listens to My voice."**

And Pilate said to Him, "Truth. Veritas. Quid est Veritas? What is truth?"

Jesus answered, **"Ego sum Veritas - I am Truth."**

Then Pilate summoned the Chief Priests and the Elders

to him, saying to them, "You have brought this Man to me and have accused Him of inciting the people to revolt. I have conducted my investigation and have not found Him guilty of the charges you brought against Him."

The Chief Priests and the Elders began to argue among themselves, and then one of the Elders called out to Pilate, "Begging the Prefect's pardon, but please hear our concerns. This Jesus has been inciting the people and refuses to listen to our lawful decrees. He has been inciting nothing but rebellion since He came here from Galilee. Even in Galilee, He has been fomenting rebellion and he has continued to do the same all the way to here in Jerusalem."

Hearing that Jesus came from Galilee, he asked the Chief Priests and the Elders, "You say that this Jesus has been inciting the people since He came here from Galilee? Is this Jesus a Galilean?"

"Yes, Prefect, He is."

"Then, if that is the case," replied Pilate, "this Man comes under the jurisdiction of Herod. Herod is here in Jerusalem, so I order you to take this Man to Herod for judgment." With that, Pilate went back inside the Praetorium.

The Temple guards dragged Jesus away from Pilate's palace and headed toward Herod's Palace. Declan, Tomy, and Nick were part of the crowd following Jesus to Herod's Palace; Antoine and Sam joined them as part of the crowd, with Ray and John trailing well behind them. The rest of the team maintained their location outside Fortress Antonia and waited for orders.

Herod's Palace

Herod, the Tetrarch of Galilee, and Perea heard that Jesus would be brought before him for judgment. Earlier, he had imprisoned and eventually executed Jesus' kinsman, John the Baptizer, and now he had become interested in Jesus and who He might be. Some had speculated that John the Baptizer had risen from the dead, and Herod hoped that Jesus might perform some sign to indicate who He was.

"Oh, yes, so who do we have here? Jesus of Nazareth," Herod put down his wine. "I am the 'fox' of whom you spoke." Jesus did not say a word. Then, speaking to the Chief Priests and Elders, Herod said, "Tell me why you brought me this Man."

"He is fomenting hate and dissent in the streets, Tetrarch, and as a Galilean, He falls under your jurisdiction."

"Very well. Then let me question our accused. Tell me, Rabbi, what have You to say to your accusers?"

Jesus did not answer him. Herod posed many questions to Jesus for well over an hour, and Jesus did not utter a word in reply.

"Can you not see, Tetrarch? He is mocking and disrespecting you with His silence. He continues to demonstrate His disdain for your rightful and lawful authority as much as He refuses to recognize our moral authority. He must account for His crimes, and our people cry out for justice!" The Chief Priests and Elders continued in this vein, riling up Herod and his soldiers.

"Rabbi, if you do not answer me, I will have no choice but to send you back to the Roman Governor, for he can dispense the appropriate punishment. But I would much rather keep this issue within our authority. What do you have to say to Your accusers?" Jesus continued to maintain His silence, further antagonizing Herod.

"What are You? Are You mad? I have given You the opportunity to benefit from my mercy, and how do You pay me back? By insulting me!"

At this, Herod's soldiers joined in with the Chief Priests and Elders in abusing Jesus. Herod became bored with this, so he ordered the Chief Priests and Elders to take Him back to Pilate for punishment.

"But first, let us send this Man back to Pilate attired in garb that suits His station." The soldiers wrapped Jesus in a royal purple robe and sent Him back to the Roman Governor. Declan and the other team members saw Jesus being taken into Herod's Palace, and after an hour and a half or so, they saw the guards take Jesus in the direction of Pilate's headquarters. Declan contacted Jonathan and the other team members at the Antonia Fortress to tell them what was happening.

"We'll be trailing this crowd to Pilate's headquarters, and then we'll start dispersing our team as this group heads out to the hill of Calvary; let me know if anything shakes loose where you are, out."

Pilate's Headquarters

The crowd was very agitated when they arrived at Pilate's Praetorium. Pilate left his residence and addressed the Chief Priests, the Elders, and the crowd standing in the *Gabbatha*. Pilate began by repeating what he had told them earlier, "I have told you all that I have conducted my investigation and have not found Him guilty of the charges that you have brought against Him. You sent Him to Herod for judgment, and Herod has sent Jesus back to me; it is obvious that He is not guilty of the charges you have levied against Him. But to teach Him a lesson not to involve Himself with you, I will have Him flogged and then release Him." The crowd became even more incensed, and they cried out for Jesus to be crucified. Pilate continued to waver as he remembered his wife's admonition. To placate this crowd that was becoming increasingly hostile, Pilate said, "I still find no guilt in this Man, but I am familiar with one of your customs that allows me to release one prisoner to you during your Passover. Whom shall I release to you?" The crowd cried out as one to release the revolutionary and murderer, Barabbas, to them. Pilate did not think that the crowd would accept Barabbas as they knew who he was and what crimes he committed; he was still convinced that there was no guilt with Jesus, and he thought that if he were to scourge Jesus, he might placate the crowd. He ordered his soldiers to take Jesus to the Antonia Fortress and have punishment meted out.

Declan and the team members outside of Pilate's palace heard all that was happening. Tomy looked at Declan and said,

"Pilate is still wavering; he cannot find Jesus guilty of the crimes that Caiaphas and the rest have accused Him of. His wife must have really put the fear in him."

Ray, a Coptic Christian, added, "She is the only one who tried to intervene for Him with Pilate. She is venerated as a saint and martyr in Egypt but couldn't stop what was happening. I can't believe what we're seeing." The crowd moved off to the Fortress.

Chapter Fourteen
His Passion

The purple cloak Jesus wore was removed, and He was tied to a post in a punishment area outside of the soldiers' barracks. Two Roman soldiers on either side of Him, each armed with a flagellum. Each of these two flagella was a sharp whip with metal barbs at the end for inflicting maximum pain and damage to the flesh, not to mention what horrible damage they could do to an eye. Declan, Tomy, Jonathan, Ray, and the other team members were observing the rest of the crowd that had gathered outside of the courtyard. Along with the many onlookers who were screaming for Jesus' punishment and crucifixion, many in the crowd were screaming for His release. Tomy and Nick were mingling through the crowd and hearing what the people were saying. Many people were looking at Jesus as a prophet, and some claimed that He was the Messiah promised to them. But then the scourging began, and it was a horrible sight to behold. With each lash of the flagellum, huge chunks of flesh were ripped out, and Jesus began to bleed profusely from His many wounds. It appeared as if He may have passed out due to the pain, but one could hear soft moaning coming from His mouth. Mercifully, the scourging stopped, and the soldiers pulled Him from the post and led Him back inside Pilate's Praetorium. Once inside, the soldiers threw the purple cloak over Him and began to mock Him, spitting on Him and hurling insults at Him. One of the soldiers took a branch of thorns and weaved it into a crown. The soldier placed this on Jesus' head and then pushed the crown down, cutting into His scalp. The soldiers began to mock Him mercilessly, chanting, "All Hail the King of the Jews!" After they tired of this game of theirs, they brought Him back to Pilate.

Pilate's wife, Claudia, was with him inside the praetorium, and she told him once again, "You have to release this Man. He is not guilty of any crime. Caiaphas and those other vipers are manipulating you because they don't have the guts to do this themselves, always hiding behind their religion." With that, she left in disgust. She went into her residence inside the praetorium and changed her clothes.

The soldiers took Jesus inside the Praetorium and had Him stand before Pilate. Pilate looked at the horrible scourge marks on Jesus, and he was sickened at the sadism with which the soldiers inflicted their punishment. Jesus was bleeding from His wounds and could barely stand. With a gentle touch, Pilate eased Jesus to the edge of the praetorium overlooking the *Gabbatha*. He still wanted to show the crowd that he could find no guilt in Jesus.

"Here, I am bringing this Man out to show Him to you and to announce once again that I find no guilt in Him. *Ecce Homo*, behold the Man."

The crowd was screaming for Pilate to crucify Him. Pilate answered them, "Take Him yourselves. I find no fault with this man." He approached Jesus and asked Him, "Where are you from?" When Jesus did not answer him, Pilate said, "Do you not speak to me? Do you know that I have the power to release you and the power to crucify you?"

Jesus answered, **"You have no power over Me if it had not been given to you from above. For this reason, the one who handed Me over to you has the greater sin."**

Pilate was still hesitant to condemn Jesus, and he tried to release Him once again, but the crowd cried out again, "If you release Him, you are not a friend of Caesar. Everyone who makes himself a king opposes Caesar." The crowd continued to scream out for Pilate to crucify Jesus. Pilate asked once again, "What evil has He done?" But the crowd screamed even louder to crucify Jesus. Pilate realized that he had a riot about to occur, took water and a bowl, and washed his hands in front of the crowd. He told the crowd, "I am innocent of this Man's blood; look to this yourselves."

The crowd yelled, "His blood be on us and on our children!" Pilate handed Jesus over to be crucified. As soon as the order was given for Jesus' execution, Declan deployed the team to various areas along the street to observe Jesus' walk to His crucifixion.

"Kevin, Jonathan, and Josh get yourselves in position by the Gate of Ephraim and follow the crowd as it proceeds to head west. Jerry and John move over to the Judgment Gate. It's right before the hill of Calvary. Go ahead and blend in with the crowd as it moves onto the hill. The rest of us will be working our way west. Everyone listen up; things are moving rapidly right now and can change instantly. Be prepared to fall back if things get too hairy with this crowd; we don't want any of us to get injured. We will see something here that will affect us all, remain objective, and focus on our mission. We all know what we're supposed to do and how we're supposed to act. Stick to our training, and we'll be on our way back to the Central Mountains in a couple of days. Just hang in there, Guys."

Outside of the Praetorium, standing on the *Gabbatha* with Jesus, were two criminals who were also being led out to be crucified. The Roman soldiers placed the heavy wooden cross on Jesus' shoulders, and they put the cross beams across the shoulders of each of the criminals. Jesus was placed in the lead position, and they began the slow, mournful march to the hill of Calvary, called Golgotha in Aramaic, the place of crucifixion. Jesus was visibly struggling to carry this cross, and He was subjected to continual beatings by the soldiers and insults from the crowd. Declan, Tomy, and Nick were following Jesus and the two criminals. Antoine, Sam, Ray, and John had leapfrogged ahead and had blended in with the crowd. Slowly and deliberately, they were following this sad procession out of the city, which wound its way from the Praetorium through the Antonia Fortress and the streets of Jerusalem heading west.

Jesus and the two criminals walked through the street, a cobblestone pavement made uneven by the amount of foot and cart traffic through the years. A Roman soldier on horseback was leading Jesus and the other condemned men, with soldiers walking alongside to keep the crowd in check. Within minutes of passing through the Fortress, Jesus fell on the street under the weight of the cross. The procession stopped, and one of the Roman soldiers started to beat Jesus with a whip. Nick, who was very close to the edge of the crowd, could see all of this very clearly. He balled his fists and was ready to jump into the street until Declan and Tomy put their hands on his shoulders to restrain him. Tomy looked at Nick and very calmly said to him in Greek, 'σταμάτα,'— stamata, which means 'stop.' Nick came to his senses and stopped, but he was still wound as tight as a spring. Without a word, the three men blended back into the crowd.

The crowd itself was completely out of control, and if not for the Roman guard detail, the crowd would have taken matters into their own hands. Once again, Temple Guards blended in with the crowd and continually provoked everyone. In addition to yelling and screaming at Jesus, some in the crowd were throwing stones at Jesus and the two criminals. One of the Roman guards saw this and hit the offender across his head with the soldier's pilum. "Do not interfere with our performing our duty!" The crowd was stunned momentarily, but no one threw any more stones after that.

Jesus continued His slow and agonizing journey to Golgotha, and along His way, He stopped. Standing before Him close to the Gate of Ephraim was His mother. His mother recalled the words that Simeone said to her years ago, that a sword would pierce her heart. She could feel the sword piercing her as she looked at her beloved Son in His agony. Jesus was exhausted to the point of collapse, but when He looked at His mother, He could feel her strength and her love for Him, which gave Him the strength to continue on His fateful path.

The Roman soldier, he too had a mother, in a moment of sympathy and compassion, allowed Jesus to linger for a moment while Jesus looked into His mother's eyes. After a short time, the young soldier prodded Jesus into moving. Shortly after this, Jesus' strength was completely spent and He had difficulty finding His footing on the uneven pavement. The same young soldier saw this and looked into the crowd. Seeing a worker dressed as a field laborer, the soldier grabbed this man and told him to help Jesus carry His cross. The man was at first reluctant to help, but with a Roman pilum thrust into his face, he had no choice. This man, his name was Simon, helped to lift the cross off of Jesus' shoulders, and when he looked into Jesus' weary and struggling eyes, Simon saw a look of humility and gratitude; his reluctance stopped right there. He helped to carry Jesus' cross for a couple of hundred meters until the soldier on horseback said, "Enough!" Simon gently placed the heavy, wooden cross back upon Jesus' shoulders. As soon as Jesus accepted this load, He fell again. Simon reached down and tried to help Jesus back onto His feet, but the Roman soldier grabbed Simon by his tunic and pulled him away.

Jesus struggled further down the street, and at a slight turn before the Judgment Gate, the slow procession was stopped by a group of women who were wailing and crying. The young Roman soldier went over to force Jesus to continue, but as soon as he looked into the group of women, he stopped cold and moved back. Jesus began to talk to this group of women who knew Jesus and had heard His words of love and forgiveness. One of the women stepped forward, and very gently, she took her veil and wiped Jesus' face. After a moment, Jesus continued His way. The young Roman soldier looked back at the group of women. He had a feeling that he knew one of them, that he had seen her face before. He was looking for the woman he saw in the crowd, and there, he saw her. She was dressed as all of the other women were dressed, but he looked at her one last time to be sure; there was no doubt who she was; he saw the unmistakable face of Claudia Procula, the Prefect's wife; she was wailing and crying with the rest of the women.

Jesus looked up from His load and saw that He would have to ascend the rise up to Golgotha. His strength gave out one last time, and He fell again to the ground. This time, the soldiers showed no patience and began to whip Jesus mercilessly. Nick and Tomy could not contain themselves at this time and were ready to jump into the street. Declan, who by this time was joined by other team members, yelled aloud, "Stamata!" Jonathan and Josh grabbed Nick and Tomy and pulled them back. Others in the crowd did not even notice this going on as they were still yelling and cursing Jesus and the two criminals. With the noise going on with the crowd, Declan, obviously distressed by what was happening, leaned over to Nick and Tomy and told them, "Stand down, you two. We cannot and will not interfere with what is happening. We'll be out of here soon. Just hold on. We will watch this to the end and then return to the house."

Agonizingly slow, Jesus made His way to the crest of the small hill, and He was ordered to drop His cross. The crowd of people began to inch their way closer to the spot where Jesus was, and they began to berate Jesus even more loudly. The crowd's mood was getting uglier and angrier by the second, and you could feel the hostility growing. Jesus was stripped of His clothing and ordered to lie on the cross. The crowd, seeing that Jesus was entirely under the power of the Romans, began to yell at Him again. "How dare You call Yourself our King! Look at You now! You blasphemer, You told us all that You're going to rebuild the Temple. You can't even care for Yourself!" And with that, they all jeered and spat at Him.

Nick and Tomy were both very shaken, witnessing the abuse that Jesus was subjected to, as were all of the members of the team, but they knew that they could not interfere. But by this time, a change appeared to have happened to Declan as he was watching the Romans prepare Jesus for crucifixion; it was as if he had been debating something in his mind and then came to a decision. Declan told Tomy to pass the word to the team to stand by and be ready to act at a moment's notice. Tomy asked him, "What are you planning on doing? You know we can't affect any changes with what's happening here. We have to let this play out."

Declan replied, "Just stand by. I know what will happen, but think about it, Tomy, we can't let anyone else interfere. I know this has to play out, but I don't want any of His followers to start thinking that they're going to pull a John Wayne and think that they're the cavalry coming to the rescue. We have to let this continue, but we can't let anyone interfere with this and take matters into their own hands." With that, Tomy nodded his assent and began to make his way to the team members to let them know what was going to happen. Tomy sidled up to Nick and began to speak to him in Greek; that got him a few glances, but as there were many Greek pilgrims in the city for Passover, it wasn't too far out of the ordinary.

By this time, all of the team members were at the top of the hill where Jesus was going to be crucified, and they all knew what Declan had passed on to Tomy. They were going to stand by until they got the command to take action. They were all still mixed in with the crowd, observing the crowd and keeping their eyes on Jesus, but Declan began to move forward with Ray and Tomy right at his side. The two thieves were the first to be crucified, but the crowd gave little notice to their screams. There was a rumbling in the crowd as the Roman soldiers began to nail Jesus to the Cross, and then screams of "Crucify Him!" began to reverberate through the crowd. It was as if all of their hatred and anger began to focus on Jesus.

All who were near His Cross could feel the agony that Jesus was experiencing. Declan moved even closer, only to be pushed back by one of the soldiers. Jesus was erected on His Cross, and you could hear His flesh tearing as His weight settled. His agony was horrible to see and hear. But instead of the crowd showing some semblance of compassion to this Holy Man, they became even more angered and began pushing towards the Cross. Some started to hurl stones at Jesus in an attempt to kill Him before the Cross could. The crowd became even more incensed and began to push at the Roman line that was set up. Declan knew that the crowd would probably tear Jesus down from the Cross and take matters into their own hands. Declan looked at the crowd and noticed for the first time that two women and a young man were standing at the foot of the Cross. They appeared to be the only ones who were not mocking Jesus, and when Declan looked at one of the women, he noticed that it was Jesus' mother. She raised her head, and with tears in her eyes, she looked directly at Declan; he could see the pleading in her eyes to help her Son. The noise from the crowd exploded once again with pure hatred for Jesus on the Cross, and as one, the crowd moved toward the Cross and pushed the Roman guards back. Declan knew that this was it. The crowd was going to tear Jesus down from the Cross and kill Him themselves. He pulled a flash-bang from his pack and threw it toward the crowd. The flash-bang had the desired effect and stopped the crowd in their tracks. Declan and Ray pushed their way through the stunned Roman guards and ran to the foot of the Cross. Ray had his modified HK MP7a1 submachine gun out and fired a quick burst of non-lethal rounds into the ground very close to the soldiers' feet. Ray's burst stopped the soldiers in their tracks, just as Declan's flash-bang did with the crowd. Immediately after the crowd and the soldiers halted where they were, they fell prostrate on the ground. The only ones who remained standing were the mother of Jesus and the two people with her. They were all frozen with fear. At that moment, the remaining team members rallied to Declan's side, and they surrounded the crucified Christ in a circle with their weapons at the ready. The crowd kept their faces to the ground, but the Roman soldiers quickly got up and assumed defensive postures. They were as terrified as the Jews.

There was no noise. There was no screaming. It was deathly quiet. Quiet. You could feel, but not hear, the wind moving over the Hill of Calvary. Then, out of the quietude, you could hear the agonized breathing of the three men on their crosses. One of the young Roman soldiers who was part of the crucifixion detail looked over at his comrade. "Why is it so quiet? We have done hundreds of these crucifixions, if not more, but I have never heard it like this. We've done something wrong, haven't we?"

"Be still," his comrade hissed at him. "Don't say

another word. The angels may think that we are dead and leave us be."

Tomy began to yell in Aramaic, asking who was in charge, "*Manile meshtlana akha?*" The crowd of onlookers and Romans remained silent. Tomy began to yell at them, asking if they understood him, and one of the women at the cross answered with her face still down on the ground, "Yes, we understand you, and we know who you are. You are the angels the Teacher said would come down to protect Him. How can we answer you; how can we speak to angels of the Lord Most High?" The crowd was completely silent.

The rapid turn of events began to spin rapidly out of control, but Declan continued to survey the crowd while keeping an eye on Jesus on the cross. Both he and Tomy were overwhelmed by emotion as a lifetime of Christian teaching was hurtling out of them. As a Chaldean and caught up in what he was experiencing, Tomy was the hardest hit in the group. Declan was struggling with what he was dealing with. He knew that he had to accomplish his mission, but he was looking at Jesus dying on the Cross and could not take it all in. He was visibly shaken by the vision of Jesus being crucified, and he told Tomy to ask Jesus what they could do to get Jesus down from the Cross and to safety. Tomy was utterly overcome with emotion and anguish as he was looking at Jesus being crucified. Tomy had a difficult time maintaining his composure and began to weep.

The people in the crowd were all still low to the ground, and the Roman soldiers were slowly backing up, but now they were all looking at Jesus on the Cross and listening to Him talk with Declan and the team. They were still terrified, but now they were confused as they saw one of "the angels" weeping as he was talking to Jesus. They could not understand what was happening.

"*Mari w Alahi*," Tomy said to Jesus in Aramaic, "my Lord and my God!" He continued in Aramaic, "We are here to save You from this horrifying death. Please tell us what to do."

The rest of the group laid down more suppressive fire to keep everyone at bay as they prepared to rescue Jesus from the Cross. Things began to spiral out of control quickly as Tomy looked up and began speaking to Jesus. Jesus looked down at the team and said in perfectly accented American English.

"Declan, Tomy, all of you, My brothers, I know why you are here, and I know what you are attempting to do. You must know, and you must understand that I have to accept this physical death as atonement for you all. I have to fulfill the will of My Father."

Declan and Tomy were unable to process this. Declan looked at Tomy and Ray and said *sotto voce* "How can this be? How can He know who we are? You heard Him as clearly as I did. How can He speak English? English has not even been developed at this time?"

But in an instant, it erased any of their doubts about who was upon the Cross: They were in the presence of the Son of the Living God, the God of Abraham, Isaac, and Jacob. They were in the presence of Jesus the Christ, the Redeemer of the World. They were in the presence of God Himself.

Looking back up at Jesus, Declan answered, "Yes, Lord, but I cannot stand to see this happening to You. Haven't you suffered enough? Can't the suffering that You have already endured pay for our sins? Isn't just one drop of Your blood sufficient to take away our sins and the sins of the whole world?"

Jesus replied, **"No, Declan, you must know that perfect love requires a perfect sacrifice. You all know what has to be done. Your work is done here. Just know that I love you and will always be with you. Now go. I will be with you every step of the way as you make your way back to your own time and your own home."**

Declan and Tomy could not take this in. They would have to abandon their Lord and their God to this crowd. They could not make themselves leave. But Jesus said again, **"It is almost finished. Leave these people; they do not know what they have done, but they will. You all must be My witnesses to the people of your time. You know what you have to do."**

Jonathan, who had been witnessing all of this, could feel

4,000 years of Jewish history burst in his soul. This Jesus, Yeshua, was a Holy Rabbi, there was no doubt, but when Jonathan heard Jesus speaking English to Declan and Tomy and what He said to them, he could not process it. But his soul was on fire, and he looked up at the Crucified Christ, and without even thinking, he began to recite the Shema:

Sh'ma Yisra'eil Adonai Eloheinu Adonai Echad!
Baruch shem k'vod malkhato le'olam va'ed.
V'ahav'ta eit Adonai Elohekha m'odekha
b'khol l'vav'kha uv'khol naf sh'kha.
uv'khol m'odekha

After Jonathan prayed the Shema and uncovered his eyes, he looked up at Jesus and heard Him reciting the Shema with him. Jonathan felt as if he were ready to burst with a kinship he had never known for a fellow man. He then heard something that he had not heard in years; he heard this Man suffering this excruciating death begin to pray the Psalms, and he heard the 22nd Psalm being prayed, **"Eli, Eli, lema sabachthani? My God, My God, why have you forsaken Me?"** And with that, Jesus looked out and said, **"I thirst."**

The centurion whose servant was healed by Jesus cautiously approached Declan and Jonathan and, in a very humble and terrified voice, asked what he could do to help them. "I know this Man, and I know that He has done no wrong. He is a Holy Man and a Good Man. He saved my brother from death; I must help Him; what can I do?" The centurion looked past Declan and Jonathan and saw Tomy. "Don't I know you? Who are you?" The recognition began to dawn on him, "Yes, I know who you are. You asked me about Larus. Why are you here, and what language are you speaking with the preacher Yeshua? What kind of weapons are those?" This time, a flash of understanding came over the centurion's face, and he recalled what the woman said at the foot of the Cross. "You are the angels who have come to save Yeshua!" Fear came over the centurion, and he was unable to move.

161

Declan told the centurion to get something to drink for The Lord to slake His thirst. This shook the centurion out of his stupor, and he ordered one of his soldiers to get some wine for Yeshua to drink. The centurion got a sponge and plunged it into a jug of wine. Taking a pilum, he put the sponge up to Jesus' mouth and offered him a drink. The sponge dropped to the ground, and Tomy picked it up without thinking about it and put it into his bag.

After Jesus had taken the wine, he looked up to His Heavenly Father and cried out, **"Father, into Your hands I commend My Spirit."** And with that, He breathed His last.

The centurion asked what else he could do; he needed to do something, perform some penance for his role in executing Jesus. The centurion was beside himself with grief, and he yelled out in a loud voice, "We have killed an innocent man! Truly, this Man is the Son of God!" And with that, the centurion fled.

Declan looked at Jesus, who had passed on to His Father. Declan and Tomy recalled what Jesus told them, to be His witnesses. This gave them the strength to carry on. Declan knew that they had to get back and report what had occurred. The team gathered around Declan, and he outlined what they would do: "According to our calculations, the TLP is going to reopen in less than 40 hours; we have to get back to the coastline. Antoine and Sam return to the house and grab Dapples and the cart. Meet us at the Horse Gate in exactly one hour. Also, make sure that we do not leave anything behind. Let's move out of here slowly and not make any waves. Keep your eyes open and make sure that we're not tailed."

As they looked around, they noticed that the crowd was still very quiet, and then they noticed that the sky was becoming very dark. Looking up, they could see that the moon was eclipsing the sun. Upon seeing this, the crowd became terrified and began to scream. Declan thought that this might give them the opportunity to escape from this place, so they began to move away from the foot of the Cross. The plan was to move away from the crowd but try to appear as normal as possible and look like any other small group of men leaving this small hill. As they began their slow and cautious attempt to extricate themselves from Calvary, they felt they could break unnoticed. But some young men in the crowd took a special interest in "the angels" and noticed this slow withdrawal on the part of the team. The team continued to blend in with the crowd and move as slowly as not to arouse any suspicion. They made it look like they were melting back into the crowd, but as the young men watched the team's movements, there was no doubt they were actually trying to get away.

These young men began to ask each other, "Who are these men? Listen to them. What language are they speaking? What are those weapons they have with them? Some say these men are the Lord's angels, but why are they sneaking away? Angels wouldn't do this; they might be Roman Soldiers or worse, agents of Satan." Either way, they felt this group of foreigners needed to be followed.

After about an hour or so, they had made it back toward the city's wall, and before they began to make their way northeast on the road to Bethesda, Declan had Antoine and Sam let Dapples loose. There were herds of wild donkeys in the hills, and there were also farmers who would gladly take another beast of burden. Dapples would not be alone for long. The team then took all of the remaining gear that they could use from the cart and left behind whatever they couldn't. The cart and all of the remaining equipment had to be burned so as to not leave any evidence of the team being in Jerusalem. Their plan was to walk northeast for a mile and then they would gradually head west towards the Central Mountains; by all outward appearances, they were still a group of pilgrims.

Ray approached Declan and Tomy and reported, "Listen, there are about fifteen or so locals who have been shadowing us ever since we left Calvary, and it looks as if they have followed us out of town. I dropped back a bit to see and there's no doubt about it, we're being followed. These guys don't appear to be just local farmers or shepherds. They're using some pretty good field craft in keeping an eye on us; they might be pretty well organized."

"OK, good job, Ray. Have one of our guys watch our back door and one of our guys take point. Let's just do this slow and easy, we don't want to hurt anyone."

Chapter Fifteen

Declan began to think as they continued their way out of Jerusalem. Now, they had company. All they wanted to do was get back to the Central Mountains, get their vehicles, head to the coast, and wait until the Portal opened. Now these locals might slow them down a bit. They would have to see what would happen. Tomy approached Declan and asked him, "Who do you think these guys are?"

Declan replied, "I don't know, they could be anybody. They could be some of the revolutionaries, they could be Zealots, they could be any number of groups. I just want to have a smooth hike back to the mountains to get some rest and catch the TLP. Who do you think that they are?"

Tomy thought about that and said, "My money's on the fact that they're Zealots. Remember them? They were the defenders of the faith and wanted to overthrow their Roman overlords. They wanted an armed revolt against Rome, and I bet you that they heard us talking, and they think we're part of a Roman team. Nick and I talked with that centurion, and he fought against the Zealots. He said that they're pretty tough, and from what he told me, they have a good lay of the land and know how to use hit-and-run tactics. We need to keep that in the back of our minds."

"OK, good call, so we'll keep an eye on them and see how froggy they want to get. We should be able to make some good time seeing how it's pretty dark already; as long as this eclipse holds out, we should be good. It's almost night anyway this time of year." The team continued their way west.

Tomy was quiet and very thoughtful as they made their way to the Central Mountains, but he opened up after a long while to Declan. "Deck, what happened back there? For the longest time, you kept telling us to focus on the mission and not interfere, but what happened? What changed with you?"

"As I said back there, it looked as if the crowd was ready to take Jesus down from His Cross and kill Him right there. We couldn't let that happen. You're the classicist; what do you know about crucifixions? How many of them ended up with the condemned man being torn off of the cross and torn apart by an angry crowd?"

Tomy thought about what his friend had said. "Are you going to stick to that explanation? That's bullshit, and you know it. What happened to you?"

Declan was trying his best to maintain his composure. "I couldn't stand seeing Him suffer like that. I couldn't take it anymore. All of my training and everything I worked for went out the window; I acted purely on emotion. I know that our mission has been a success from an official standpoint. We observed Jesus of Nazareth and will report what we saw, but I know in my innermost being that I blew the mission. I interfered."

"Deck, we almost interfered with the natural course of history and the natural order of things. Look at how everything could have changed; all that we know throughout history could have changed. Look at the ethical implications of what we did back there. I don't know, I'm just confused, and I'm venting on you, but it's haunting me; everything in the future could have changed."

"You're right, Tomy. Everything could have changed, but it won't. He made sure of that. And He also told us that He would make sure that we would get back home safely. He has a plan for us, Tomy."

The team spread out as they were in open country and

remained vigilant. The mountains lay about 15 miles to the west. They took a quick break, and Declan had a chance to brief everyone. "We should be able to make the rally point and get our rolling stock in another couple of hours. If we make contact with any locals, try not to engage them if at all possible. Our ROE state that we are to avoid any casualties, so if we start to mix it up, just lay down suppression fire and stay concealed. How much ammo do we have left?"

Ray had already taken an inventory of everything and said, "When we were laying down our suppression fire back at Calvary, we used up quite a bit of what we had on hand. We have about 400 rounds left. Jonathan has some of his sniper rounds left over."

Jonathan had his Mk 13 Sniper Rifle and had about 60 rounds of ammunition left. They were a bit low on ammunition, so their best option was to avoid contact as much as possible. Declan piped up again, "If anyone sees anything, radio me immediately, and let's see if we can be invisible. My thoughts are that we can have Jonathan hold them off as far away as possible; that way, we won't have to get into it at all. OK, let's check all of our gear and in about five mikes let's move out."

About an hour later, Nick, who was acting as the team's tail, reported to Declan that he had some significant activity several miles back. A group of locals were heading their way, and they were in a hurry. Within a few moments, Ray got a heads up from Kevin, who was walking point, that there was a group ahead of them in the foothills; it looked as if they were trying to set up an ambush on the team. Declan ordered the team into three smaller elements so as not to concentrate their numbers, but they were still close enough to each other to offer support as needed. They planned to avoid contact as much as possible and to meet up at the rally point. Their only concern was that if the locals were Zealots, there was a strong possibility of a confrontation.

Ray received another report that although the team had done their best to avoid the ambush setup, it looked as if the ambush team was mirroring their movements. Declan had the groups maneuver to flank the ambush group and hopefully force them into keeping their heads down with suppression fire. But Declan got a call from Nick that the group on their tail had closed the distance significantly, and they could expect some contact soon. Declan decided they had enough time to wait this out, so he ordered the team to conceal themselves and avoid all contact with the tracking group.

They hid, and in about thirty minutes, the group trailing them ran right by them. They tracked them with their NVGs and noticed they were heading right towards the ambush group west of them. The two groups were going to collide with each other in the dark. As the trailing group ran into the ambush group, there was some screaming and confusion, but they identified each other quickly. Kevin got back to Declan and told him that whoever was following them must have realized that they must have missed them, so they regrouped. It looked like they were going to backtrack and try to find them.

The team quietly began to move in a southerly direction, hoping they could evade their pursuers. They would hunker down for a bit if they could get away from them and then make it to the rally point. Declan estimated they had about thirty hours until the TLP opened up. Once they got their vehicles, they could reach the TLP point in less than an hour. They had some time, but Declan did not want to risk missing the TLP opening.

They were able to low crawl out of the area away from the ambush group and were able to see the group through their NVGs heading in the opposite direction. Declan had the team pick up the pace a bit, and they made it to the Central Mountain rally point in under an hour. The vehicles and everything were in good condition, and as they were in a well-concealed location, Declan decided to hole up for a bit and head to the coast under cover of darkness. He called Tomy over and asked, "What do you think? I know that our mission is to be classified for a number of years, but we have to talk to somebody about this. I mean, it's all true. People have to know! Edgeton and his group of brainiacs will try to discount everything we have seen, but why did the portal open up a week ago? You know what the "cosmic event" was as well as I do. When Jesus raised Lazarus from the dead, that opened the portal. And why do you think we're scheduled to get out of here tomorrow morning? What's tomorrow morning, Tomy? Easter Sunday. The cosmic event is going to be His Resurrection. That's going to open the portal. Tomy, you saw Him, He talked to us. How could He speak in English? Remember what I said when we were there? 'English isn't even around yet..' How could He talk to us and know who we were? Tomy, that was God on the Cross. It's all true. We have to tell everyone. I realize that we're all like 'Doubting Thomas' and that he had to have physical proof in order to believe, but what are we? We're the proof. There is no way that they can look at the twelve of us and tell us that we're all nuts."

Tomy thought about this and said, "What did He tell us? He told us that we are to be His witnesses to our people. I think that I have my marching orders. I know what I have to do. We will have to be like the Apostles and spread the word. Look at what the Apostles did. What proof did they have besides their faith? We can do the same thing, Deck."

"Tomy, listen, we have done something impossible. We have traveled through time, and we have gone back to witness personally what Jesus has done. But Edgeton and those guys will eat us alive. They're all empiricists and need something concrete, something tangible that we can give them to test and evaluate. What artifacts did we bring back with us, the shekels? What else did we get? I know that Ray was able to pick up a gladius that one of the soldiers had dropped back at Calvary. That and the shekels have to prove that we made it through the time portal, check with the guys, and see if anyone has any other artifacts. One of those geniuses back in Pasadena can analyze that stuff and show that it's authentic. If we bring back proof that we made it through the portal, they'll have to give us at least the benefit of the doubt when we talk about Jesus."

"I don't know, Deck; I don't think trying to convert Edgeton is where we should focus our energies, at least not right now; we'll get him later. Jesus told us what He wants us to do.

As I said, I know what I will do when we get back; believe me, I know we'll make it home. He told us that we would. And I'll check with the guys to see if anyone brought some stuff back with them."

Declan thought about this. "Yeah, you're right. Right now, we should concentrate on getting everyone back home safely. Speaking of the guys, what's the sentiment with everyone?"

"I've talked with all of the other guys. They're still walking around in a state of disbelief. Then you ought to hear Jonathan. He has not stopped praying since Jerusalem. This is another St. Paul coming up. Jonathan said that he will still be able to be a Jew and be a believer in Jesus; he's on fire, Deck. Josh is also a Jew, and he is stunned, but nothing like Jonathan. I think Jonathan had a special connection with Our Lord. Have you had a chance to talk with him?"

"No, not yet, but you can see that something has changed in him," Declan replied.

"No doubt. Like me, Jonathan thinks we have to tell the world what we saw. We have to figure this out. We have to figure out how to get out of our confidentiality agreement. This is too big."

"You're right, but let's get back first, OK? He told us that He would make sure that we got home. I'm not worried about us, but I am concerned about Michael and his fire team; I have no idea what could have happened to them." Declan had been concerned about his missing comrades, and now that they were close to returning home, their absence began to weigh on him. He was the team leader, and the four missing team members were his responsibility. To add to his anxiety, Michael Parvanian was a good friend of his, and they had been through a lot together; he prayed for their safety.

When darkness came, they all got into their vehicles and made their way to the coastline. It was an uneventful trip, and the team let out a collective sigh of relief; it appeared that they had eluded their pursuers; they hoped that their good fortune would hold up.

Chapter Sixteen

Pre-Dawn
The third day following the Crucifixion

Declan and the rest of the team arranged their vehicles in the predetermined positions and awaited the opening of the TLP portal. They were approximately thirty minutes from its opening, and although their anxiety should have been pretty high as they waited, they were all calm. It was approximately 0415 Local, and it was still very dark out, but they were settled in and waiting. All of the men were very calm and relaxed, and as they began to feel a bit more comfortable, they had a chance to reflect on what they had accomplished on this mission. Their feelings were probably not much different than those of the astronauts with the Mercury program following their space flights. They were given a perilous mission into an unknown arena, and at this point, they felt a strong sense that they would make it home successfully. Then, to a man, they began thinking about what they had seen on this mission. From the moment they had seen Lazarus and his family in Bethany to their time at the foot of the Cross on Golgotha, they had the opportunity to see the face of God. Then, the doubts began to set in. Could what they had seen be nothing more than an illusion? Could they all be dreaming? Were they actually transported to the first century A.D., or did this time travel play a game with their senses, and they were still on the TLP launch site in the present? No, this was too real. What happened to them was real. How else could they explain the newly minted shekels they got from the money changers in Jerusalem or the gladius that Ray picked up? How could all of them experience the same thing? No, they were not dreaming; they had made it through the time portal and were transported to Palestine in the First Century A.D. Of that, they were all certain. The countdown continued; the portal would open soon.

Then, out of nowhere, they heard screams coming from the small hills directly east of the coastline. Reflexively, they all grabbed their weapons as they looked toward the noise. Hundreds of tribesmen were pouring out of the hills carrying swords and spears. They jumped from their vehicles, took cover, and began to lay suppressive fire ahead of the attackers. The tribesmen stopped at once and fell to the ground. Then, about 100 meters to the north, another group of attackers poured out of the hills. Declan knew that he had blown it. He assumed that within the last several hours, all was quiet, and they were not followed to the coast. But he was wrong, and he was pissed at himself. He had watches set, and none of the team members saw or heard a thing. Declan thought to himself, the team had followed all of the established procedures; how could this have happened? They laid down a few bursts of fire but were trying to conserve ammunition. They had the sea to their backs, and they could very easily swim out of the area, but as they had to make the portal opening, they had to hold their ground. They were facing easily 300 seasoned fighters who did not appear to be giving up. Then, the attackers charged again. The team fired smoke grenades, and Jonathan, with his sniper rifle and night scope, was able to shoot a number of the lead attackers with non-lethal rounds; this stopped the attack for a bit; he was doing exactly what he was trained to do as a Marine Sniper, slow the enemy's ability to maneuver. They were down to their last few rounds and were in danger of being overrun when Ray began to scream, "It's the freaking cavalry!!" The team looked behind the attackers, and flying over the hills was a dune buggy with the four missing team members: Michael, Brad, Miles, and Aaron. Declan realized that they had made it through the TLP and arrived later. Michael's team drove around the left flank of the attackers, turned right, and drove directly across their front line, laying down suppressive fire and smoke grenades. This pushed the attackers back. They then lobbed several flash-bangs, which drove the attackers over the hill and back down into the desert below. Michael hopped out of the vehicle and ran up to Declan. "I have been shadowing you all for the last few hours. We landed here sometime yesterday afternoon, but I stuck around as I knew this was our return rally point. I saw all these guys tracking you a while back, and I have to tell you, these guys know how to be quiet. I thought that we might be able to make it out of here without the shit hitting the fan. I guess that I was wrong there. Let Brad and Miles make one more sweep to keep these guys' heads down. We're due to get out of here pretty soon, aren't we?"

Declan, obviously relieved at Michael's showing up and rescuing them, replied, "The portal should open within the next fifteen minutes or so; see if we can drive these guys away. We'll then set Jonathan and Nick to guard our exit and have them jump back in the vehicles right before launch. Michael, do I have a story to tell you."

Epilogue

The team made it safely back to the present time, and as soon as they were assembled at Ashdod, they were flown back to Pasadena for an out-briefing with Murray, Nate, and other senior members of the Einstein Project.

Several months back, Tomy had an opportunity to develop a relationship with Nate and asked to meet with him before the final out-brief. Tomy told Nate that he and Declan had some sensitive information that they wanted to share with him. Nate was a bit intrigued by the message that he received from Tomy. He had an idea of what the meeting would be about and was looking forward to meeting with Declan and Tomy the next day.

"Nate, Declan, and I both know that, like us, you are a Christian, and we also know of Murray's attitude towards religion. Declan and I discussed this on the way back to our landing point on the Israeli coast. We strongly feel that he and his team will discount everything we discuss in our report, but you have to hear us out."

Declan picked up the conversation from here. "Nate, like you, I studied physics and believe in observable, quantifiable data. It's like the old expression: if something exists, it has to have some mass, and if it has some mass, it can be measured. I believe that. But as a kid, I learned my catechism and believed in the Blessed Trinity. Like a lot of people I know, as I became more 'educated' in the ways of the world, my faith as a Christian began to wane a bit. But Tomy and I have to tell you, what we witnessed in Jerusalem, it's all true. Everything we believe and learn as Christians is all true."

"Declan and I were at the foot of the Cross when Jesus was crucified. We were there, and we were all overcome by emotion as we watched a good and holy Man being subjected to unbelievable torture," added Tomy. "During the height of His agony, He looked at us and spoke to us in English. He knew who we were and what we were doing there. He gave us our marching orders, too. He commissioned us to spread His gospel. It's true, all that Scripture tells us, there is a God, and God sent His only Begotten Son to save us. We have to ask to be released from our confidentiality agreement; we cannot keep this under wraps."

Nate considered all of this. It would be an understatement to say that he was "blown away" by what Declan and Tomy told him. But then again, he wasn't surprised at all. To him, this is what he expected would happen, but how can he convince his friend, Murray? "Let me ask you something. You both said that Murray and the team would discount what you may have found if what you found proved who Jesus is. I do not discount anything that you're saying. I do believe. But if you walk into this meeting and tell them what you told me, they'll tell you that you're both delusional. Other than the experiences you just shared with me, do you have any concrete evidence we can present?"

"As proclaimed in the Gospel," Tomy said, "Jesus was thirsty, and He was given a sponge full of wine to slake His thirst. Without realizing it, I picked up the sponge and brought it back. There has to be some evidence on that sponge."

Nate could not say anything. His faith as a Christian was firm, but there were times when he questioned his beliefs. The story that Declan and Tomy told him dispelled any lingering doubts that he may have had. He was as excited as a child on Christmas morning and wanted to hear more. "Humor me for a bit. What was it like being there? How were you affected? What were you thinking?"

Declan and Tomy looked at each other, and then Declan nodded his head to Tomy in a gesture telling him to continue. "When we arrived in Bethany at the house of Lazarus and his sisters, all I could think about was my family. The villagers and Lazarus' family were preparing a meal for everyone as they gathered to mourn Lazarus. The smells of lamb being roasted in olive oil, the flatbreads being baked, and the sight of cheese and wine, I felt as if I were at a funeral for one of my family members. Then, when I heard them all speaking Aramaic, it was too much for me. We then walked up to Lazarus' house and looked off to the south. We saw Jesus and His disciples heading away. I can't explain it; imagine how you would feel if someone you loved died and then one day came back to visit you; how would you feel when you saw your loved one? That's what it felt like, but much more powerful."

Declan picked it up from there. "I think that my most inexplicable moment came when we were at the foot of the Cross, and we were looking up at Jesus being crucified. He looked down at us and began to speak to us in perfect American English. He knew who we were and what we were doing; I was, and I don't want to sound overly dramatic, but the only word I can think of to describe how I felt is 'dumbfounded,' I was completely dumbfounded. But then, in a flash of revelation, I knew who He was; I mean, I always knew that Jesus died on the Cross, but looking up and seeing this Man suffering beyond imagination, I knew beyond any doubt who He was."

Nate sat there, slowly shaking his head, and said, "Fascinating. How I envy you; you have no idea what kind of gift has been given to you. But as Tomy says, you have your 'orders.' Let me think about all of this. In the meantime, thank you both for sharing this with me. I am so grateful that you two were selected for this, and I look forward to hearing from all of the team members. I will see you all this afternoon at our out-briefing."

Later in the day, with Declan and Tomy speaking for the time travelers, Nate held an out-brief with Murray and his team. Declan and Tomy presented their findings and experiences in Palestine very calmly and deliberately and discussed what happened at the foot of the Cross. The Einstein Project team was very respectful and thanked them for their efforts, but their compelling testimony notwithstanding, they were not released from their confidentiality agreement. Severe sanctions were in place if the agreement were breached. Nothing was to be reported until the specified time of declassification.

The 'Krononauts' continued with their lives for the time being. Eventually, Declan, Tomy, and Jonathan all left the military: Declan became a contemplative Cistercian monk, commonly known as the Trappists; Tomy also joined a monastic order, the Antonian Order of St. Ormizda of the Chaldeans, and moved back to Iraq. Jonathan returned to his roots as a Jew. He became fascinated with the work of the German-Jewish philosopher Edith Stein, who later converted to Catholicism and became a Carmelite nun. Later, during the Second World War, she was executed at Auschwitz and was canonized as a Catholic saint, St. Teresa Benedicta of the Cross. Jonathan felt that there might be a possibility that he could follow a similar search for the Christian faith as she did if that were what God intended, but in the meantime, the Shema was always on his lips, and he read from the Torah daily. Jonathan was happy.

Nate was never able to convince his friend Murray that what Declan and Tomy experienced was true, but after months of cajoling him, Murray relented. They took the sponge to the National Human Genome Research Institute in Bethesda, Maryland, for testing.

The sponge was analyzed, and adequate genetic material was present for testing. A karyotype test was performed to "pair and order" the chromosomes to analyze the genetic blueprint of the subject. The scientist conducting the test for them was able to determine a number of factors from the test. Examining the images of the various chromosome pairs, the scientist could state that this sample came from an individual of Semitic origin. However, as she analyzed the two sex chromosomes, the allosomes, the scientist came out of her chair. She looked at Nate and Murray, "There is something extraordinary with this sample. I have never seen anything like it. First, I make images of the autosomes for analysis and then do the sex chromosomes last. My staining and technique are correct; I've performed this same test at least a thousand times. This is very strange; let me see if this is just a fluke." She adjusted her equipment and said, "No, there it is again."

"What's there again? What are you seeing?" asked Nate, the excitement in his voice palpable.

"All of the autosomes, the genes that come from regular body cells, are perfectly normal, but looking at the two allosomes, the sex chromosomes, the X-chromosome is a perfectly normal human sex cell. But there is something very strange with the Y-chromosome, the male chromosome, handed down *unchanged* from father to son."

"What's wrong with it?" demanded Murray.

"I can't explain it, but the Y-chromosome exhibits the same behavior even after adjusting all of my equipment. You're not going to believe this."

"What?" he was almost screaming.

"It's luminescing. The Y-chromosome is glowing."

To be continued...

ACKNOWLEDGMENTS

As with almost everything I have done in my life, I have had the help and support of many people, especially my wife, Pamela, and our children, Matthew, Elisa, and Sean. In writing this book, I had the assistance of former shipmates and colleagues, and I would like to express my gratitude for their personal perspectives, technical knowledge, and expertise; the expertise is theirs, and the mistakes are mine.

To retired Navy SEAL Captain Adam Curtis, thank you for your insights into the training of America's ultimate warriors. To Corine Cuvelier and Dr. Aaron Sinner, I appreciate your recommendations. To Thair and Tomy Ismael, thank you for sharing your love of languages and allowing me to use your names. To Captain Michael O'Connor, MC, USN (Ret), Chair Emeritus, Department of Cardiothoracic Anesthesiology, The Cleveland Clinic, it's been quite a ride! To Captain Heide Stefanyshyn-Piper, retired Naval Officer and NASA Astronaut, thanks for your insights on student life at MIT.

Et Verbum caro factum est, et habitavit in nobis.

ABOUT THE AUTHOR

Jamison A. Whiteman is a retired U.S. Naval Officer, a Vietnam Era Veteran, and a Veteran of the Persian Gulf War. He and his wife, Pamela, reside in their native San Diego. Visit his website at www.jamisonwhiteman.com.